The Barrow Case

A Luca Mystery Prequel

Dan Petrosini

DAN PETROSINI
MYSTERY & SUSPENSE AUTHOR
www.danpetrosini.com

Print ISBN: 978-1-960286-15-4
Naples, FL

Chapter One

I have to tell you about the case that framed every investigation I've worked.

The saying, that something good comes out of something bad, was one I didn't quite buy into. To me, it was a way to put a good face on a terrible situation. I was all for moving forward, no matter what, but tell me, if someone dies, does it get better because a child is born? The baby was coming, either way, and it wasn't going to resurrect the dead guy.

See what I mean? Touting the infant's birth was only a way to distract people suffering from loss.

We all remember our firsts. The first time we kissed a girl or touched her in places we weren't allowed. Our first job, our first you-know-what, and especially, for a homicide detective, our first murder case.

My first case was cut-and-dried. A wife had caught her husband cheating and plunged a steak knife into his chest. No need to conduct a meaningful investigation. The woman he was in bed with witnessed it, and the wife admitted to the murder. It never felt like a solve, and though seeing a man who'd been killed in his own bed was something I'd never forget, it didn't change me.

For me, it was the second case that altered everything. For years, I was haunted by it. Even moving from New Jersey to Naples, over a decade ago, hadn't eased the pain. Thirteen hundred miles away, and it was still talking to me. Sometimes it was just a whisper, and other times, it shouted.

I tried everything, even going to see shrink about it. But nothing worked. It was like a film of the investigation had been burned into my mind. The images, especially a harrowing one of the Barrow kid, I'll be dealing with for the rest of my life.

It was a sunny Tuesday, the tenth of October, 1995, when it all started. Bob Stone hung up the phone after a short conversation. He stood, saying, "Okay, kid. Let's get moving. They found a body in Poricy Park. It's a damn teenager."

I followed my partner out the door. Officially, he wasn't my partner. Stone was a few months from retirement, and Sgt. Gesso figured teaming me up with him would speed my education.

Driving along Middletown-Lincroft Road, I made a right onto Oak Hill Road and pulled into the entrance to the park. The heavily wooded area was a two-hundred-and-fifty-acre nature preserve. Two cruisers, lights on, were blocking the footpaths. To the right, a man with a black Labrador was talking to an officer.

I didn't know the uniforms guarding the scene and chin-nodded. As Stone spoke with them, I signed us in. Before ducking under the police tape, we put on protective gear. Stone pointed. "It's that way, by the trails."

"Who found her?"

"The guy walking his dog. We got to talk to him."

We went off the trail toward a cordoned-off area. A grim-faced officer nodded. Stone went under first. I swallowed and snuck below the tape.

Stone stood five feet away from the body. "What do you see?"

What the hell kind of question was that? "A female corpse, fourteen to sixteen years of—"

"Not that. I'm talking about the scene."

The girl was on her back, one of her thick-soled shoes was missing. "She was dragged here."

"Anything else?"

"She doesn't have a pocketbook. Most girls her age never leave the house without one."

"Good catch."

"Whoever did this either robbed her or was trying to hide her identity."

"Unless she was from a wealthy family, kids her age don't carry a lot of money around."

"You're right."

"Let's see what we can learn before the medical examiner arrives."

We bent down over the body. Leaves were floating down around us. The girl wore a light, unbuttoned bomber jacket over a tie-dyed shirt, and jeans.

Stone picked a leaf off the neck of the blond-haired girl. He said, "The kid was strangled."

"Looks like a ligature of some kind was used."

He moved his finger above the neckline. "It's a wide bruise. I'm thinking a rope rather than a wire."

I found myself swallowing. "Poor kid. I can't imagine what the parents are going—"

"Now's not the time for emotions. This is a crime scene. It's not about her right now. We have to focus on the how. It'll help us with the why-and-who parts."

I didn't fully buy the strategy. It was important to know how someone took a life, but knowing as much about the victim generally led you to the killer. "I understand, so what are you thinking?"

"Killers who use weapons, say a gun or knife, are in a class by themselves. And there's a world of difference between a shooter and a murderer who stabs someone to death."

"Killing from a distance versus up close, right?"

"Yeah, a strangulation is about as close as you can get. But it's different. There's no blood. Unless the killer carried a rope with him, it could have been rage or passion induced."

"The medical examiner will be able to tell us what was used as a ligature."

"Uh-huh. Let's hope he gives us a lot more than that."

"I don't see any bruises, and with her clothes intact, it doesn't look like she was sexually abused."

"But that doesn't mean it wasn't the intent. Some sleazebag could have swept her off the trail looking to rape her. Someone might have come into the park and scared him. He strangles the girl to keep her quiet and then slips out."

Throwing theories against the wall was the currency of a homicide detective. It was a way to flesh out possibilities, and even though it could be gruesome, I found it fascinating.

"Could be."

Stone put a hand on the victim's cheek. "I'm no doctor, but I'd say she's been dead less than a couple of hours."

"In broad daylight. And in Middletown. I just can't believe it."

"Get used to it. The suburbs haven't been immune for decades. Come on, we gotta talk with the guy who found her."

Chapter Two

We stepped back into the parking lot as two patrol cars pulled up. Walking toward them, Stone said, "Let's get a search going."

I followed him. Stone said, "Listen up. We need a complete search of the area conducted. We're looking for any physical evidence you can find. The victim is missing a shoe: black, thick soled, and didn't have a pocketbook. We think they're out there somewhere. But anything you find, no matter how small, I want the location marked and the item bagged."

"Where do you want us to start?"

"I want the entire park searched. But let's start by the crime scene. Use the standard grid-search pattern. Get booties and gloves on, and be on your damn toes. The victim is a teenage girl."

The guy with the dog had on a Yankee windbreaker and was one of those guys who wore shorts no matter the time of year. His back to us, he was crouched down, petting his dog. He rose as the officer staying with him said something to him.

Stone extended his hand; I bent down and rubbed the dog's head. "I'm Detective Stone, and this Detective Luca."

"John Turner. I can't believe this."

"Tell us how you discovered the body."

"Well, me and Hershey were going for our walk. We come here every afternoon. She was acting strange; I didn't know what it was, but Hershey's a smart dog."

"What was your dog doing?" Stone said.

"She's always excited to come the park, but as soon as we got out of the car, she stopped dead in her tracks. Then she started to go in that direction." He pointed toward the area the body was. "I tried to pull the leash back, but she was tugging me along. I figured I might as well go where she wanted. I thought it was a cat or something that would take off when we got closer. Hershey loves chasing cats."

"As you were going along, did you see anything or anyone?"

"No, but I wasn't watching all over, just kind of following her."

"Any noises or sounds?"

"No, I mean, it wasn't dead quiet though. There was some wind, and we were stepping on leaves when we left the trail." He shook his head. "And then I saw . . . her . . . and tugged on the leash. I wasn't sure and didn't know what to think. At first, I thought she'd fallen. But then I knew. I mean, she was lying there with leaves on her, and her shoes were off."

"Did you touch the body?"

"Yeah, I mean, I had to see if she was alive. I didn't know if she was, so I cinched up the leash and got close. Hershey is very obedient, and I told her to sit and she listened. I went and tried to see if she had a pulse."

"Where did you check?"

"Her neck."

"How close did the dog get to the body?"

"She sat about five feet away."

It felt like Stone had asked his questions, so I jumped in, "Mr. Turner, you mentioned coming to the park each day."

"Yeah, we have our routine every afternoon."

"Have you noticed anyone unusual in the park recently?"

"You know, this place is pretty quiet. I guess that's why whoever did it came here."

"So nobody you didn't recognize?"

"Not really. Sometimes the teenagers come here to smoke or to neck, you know, but that's about it."

"Nobody you'd consider a threat?"

"It's been a while, but there was this one guy. I don't know if he was homeless or not, but I'd see him maybe once every couple of weeks. He'd carry around a bag with him. I thought it might have been everything the poor soul owned."

"When was the last time you saw him?"

"Gotta be a good two months."

"Let us have your contact information. We may have you come down and sit with a sketch artist."

"Sure, anything I can do to help."

As he was giving me his contact details, an officer trotted out of the park. He was holding an oval-shaped pocketbook.

"Detective Stone. We found this. Thought you'd like to see it right away."

He handed the bag off. "Good work. Where'd you find it?"

"About fifty yards east. Pretty close to the railroad tracks. I flagged the location."

Immediately, I pictured the killer fleeing with the kid's pocketbook. Maybe rummaging through it. He dumps the bag and escapes via a route where no one would likely see him.

I said, "Thanks. I'd appreciate it if you can walk away from the body toward where you found it and keep an eye out for anything he might have taken out of the bag."

Stone said, "I don't want anyone to know the location or even the fact the victim didn't have her pocketbook with her. Nobody, not even the press must know. Is that clear?"

"Yes, sir."

Stone looked at me, and I said, "Of course." It was a classic move. We needed to hold a detail or two from the case for ourselves. We might need to use the nonpublic information to verify a confession.

As the officer left, Stone and I walked to our car. Next to the entrance sign, I spotted a post with a plastic box attached to it, marked maps. I grabbed one. Stone was opening up the pocketbook. I hustled back as he drew something out.

"We got a name."

It was a laminated card. The kid's high school identification. Stone said, "Mary Mercury. Kid went to Middletown South."

He held out the ID. The picture matched the dead girl.

"Anything else?"

He shook his head. I didn't know it at the time, but even Stone couldn't deny things changed when a corpse had a name. I felt it too and defaulted to unfolding the map. The place had buildings on it. They were part of the Murray farmhouse.

It was on the other side of the trail, probably two hundred yards away from the body. The map also highlighted a network of trails that stretched all the way to Poricy Pond. We needed to check the entire area out.

I said, "There's a pair of buildings out that way. You want to go check it out?"

"I'd love nothing more, but we need to speak with the parents."

Ugh. By far, it was the worst part of the job.

I said, "The medical examiner just arrived. You want me to stick around? See what he says?"

"No." How could a word with only two letters dash my hopes?

Chapter Three

We'd gotten an address for the Mercury family, and it was well under a mile from Poricy Park. I didn't notice it when we first arrived, but across the street, to the right of the park's entrance, was Fairview Cemetery.

I shuddered thinking the Mercury family would have to pass it anytime they made a right out of their street. I was new to the homicide department, but my feeling was any family who lost someone, especially a child, to violence or sickness, should move out of their house. I knew I would. They were just too many memories.

My wife didn't agree with me. She said it was tantamount to trying to erase the memory of a loved one and that people took comfort in familiar surroundings. I knew nobody could forget losing a spouse or child. What they needed was distraction and less reminders. Only then, could time dull the loss.

I was hoping something, anything, would happen that required me to stay in the car as we pulled behind an SUV in the driveway. The center-hall colonial home sat on a large, tree-covered lot. It was one of hundreds of upper-middle-class homes in the quiet neighborhood. I knew within hours of our departure;

cars would crowd the street and the home would be filled with people in disbelief.

It was 4:05 p.m. when Stone hit the bell. A female voice rang out. "Hold on a minute. I'll be right there."

A late-fortyish woman opened the door. "Can I help you?"

Stone flashed a badge. "Mrs. Mercury?"

She put a hand on her chest. "Did something happen to Bob?"

"No, ma'am. Can we come in?"

"Oh, thank God."

As she stepped aside, I felt terrible that her relief would be short lived. Closing the door behind us, she said, "Oh, here comes Bob now."

"He gets home early."

"Bobby leaves the house at six a.m. to avoid the traffic. He's an electrician working on a project in the city."

"Good idea."

"What's this all about?"

"Why don't we wait until your husband comes in."

Fear flashed across her face. "Is Mary all right?"

"Can we sit somewhere?"

"What happened to Mary?"

"Take it easy, ma'am."

The front door opened, and the husband said, "Who's parked in the driveway?"

I said, "Mr. Mercury, we're with the Middletown Police Department. Why don't you and your wife sit down."

The wife said, "Something happened to Mary!"

"What?"

"Please try to be calm. Why don't you sit down, please?"

The husband went to his wife saying, "We're not sitting anywhere until you tell me what the hell is going on."

"Is your daughter, Mary, home?"

"No, so, she's all right, then?"

I pointed to the fireplace mantel. "Is that a picture of her there?"

"Yes. Why?"

"We believe we found your daughter in Poricy Park."

"Is she okay?"

"No, ma'am. We believe she was murdered."

The shriek the mother made reminded me of the shower scene in *Psycho*. It was a movie I could no longer watch because of this case.

The parents embraced each other, and the wailing was guttural. I wanted to run outside. Stone and I gave the couple time before telling them we needed to verify the identity of the body.

The husband said, "I'll do it."

"Thank you. Her body won't be available for an hour or two. I'll call you, if that's okay?"

He nodded.

Stone said, "We'll need to speak with you and your wife, ask some questions. I know it's difficult, but the sooner the better in these types of cases. Would this evening, after the ID, work for you?"

"Okay."

"We're real sorry about all this."

He shook his head.

Stone tilted his head toward the door. Before following him out, I said to the parents, "I hope you don't mind me making the suggestion, but do you have any family nearby? It might be a good idea to give them a call. As tough as this is, it helps to have people around."

The two of them looked at each other. I said, "If you want, I can come drive by and take you to the medical examiner's."

"Thanks, but we'll be okay."

"If you change your mind, just let me know."

I HUNG UP THE PHONE. I wanted to let my wife, Debra, know it was going to be a late night. Stone came into the office with a cup of coffee.

"Check on the parents. See if they have records."

"The parents?"

"Those closest to the victim are generally the ones who did it."

"I can't believe it would be the mother. You saw her."

"We're not in the business of figuring out emotional displays."

He was right to a degree, but part of what I'd learned was how to read people, to ferret out a sign they were lying. I felt I was good at it. "It ain't her."

"Probably not, but we need to check her out. And him. He said he was working. We'll have to confirm that and everything else after we talk to them."

In my mind, there was no way either one of them could have done it. I wasn't a father, and seeing the evil in my line of work, I didn't have a strong desire to be one. My dad had died when I was just a tot, but my mom, she showered me with love and protection until she passed. I didn't think I was up to her standard of parenting. Mom was taken too early, but that's another story.

"Of course."

Stone reached for the phone. He was talking to Sgt. Gesso and shaking his head. He hung up saying, "The Mercury kid's uncle is a freeholder. He already called Gesso. Told him he expects a quick resolution to the case and wants justice for his niece."

"The case is a couple of hours old. What do they expect?"

"I don't need the goddamn pressure. I'm out of here in a few months."

Chapter Four

We followed Robert Mercury home, giving him fifteen minutes to tell his wife their worst fears had been realized. It made me remember one time an old girlfriend and I were in Upstate New York skiing, and a state trooper came to the house telling me that her brother had died.

She was in the shower, and it was up to me to tell her. Not knowing what to do, I told her we had to leave right away. She kept asking me what was going on, but I told her to get in the car and I'd tell her. I waited until we got on the thruway to let her know. We had two more hours ahead of us. As you could imagine, it seemed hours longer.

A box of tissues in her lap, Mrs. Mercury was sitting in between two women, Mary's aunt and a neighbor. Mr. Mercury was gulping a glass of scotch behind the couch. We advised of our preference to speak to just the parents. As Mr. Mercury led us into the dining room, I regretted turning down the drink he offered.

We sat around an oak dining table in wooden chairs without padding. Coming from an Italian family that camped out for hours on holidays, I knew a setup like this wouldn't work for us. I took out my notebook as Stone began.

"We're real sorry about all of this, and we don't want to upset you, but we have to ask certain questions."

Mr. Mercury said, "We understand. We'll do anything we can do to help you find the bastard."

"When was the last time you saw Mary?"

The mother said, "This morning. She left for school about seven thirty."

"I was at work already, in Manhattan."

"Where do you work?"

"At Hunter Roberts. We're putting up a new tower on Sixty-Fifth Street."

"What time do you get back to Middletown?"

"You were here when I got back. What are you getting at?"

"Just answer the questions. It will be a lot easier."

I said, "As Detective Stone mentioned at the outset, some of the questions may seem unfair, but we have to ask them. So please bear with us. How did you leave the city?"

"I took the three o'clock bus out of the Port Authority."

"Thank you. Mrs. Mercury, what did your day look like after Mary went to school?"

"I did some housework and then went to Workout World around ten a.m. I got back around noon. This is all . . ." Her chin began quivering.

"Please, just bear with us a little longer. You never know what information you give us that we'll find useful."

"Useful for what? Framing us?"

"No, sir. Someone may have been watching you. Some encounter may have set off an unstable individual. I wish I could tell you what, but we just don't know. Does that make sense?"

"Okay, okay. So I went to Macy's after showering and got back around three thirty and started prepping for dinner. Then . . . then . . . you came." She dabbed her eyes.

Stone said, "Okay. Now, is there anyone you think could be responsible for this?"

"No, Mary was the perfect child. She got along with everyone."

Every parent believed their child was the model for humanity. The reality was parents either didn't know about a kid's flaws and struggles or looked the other way.

"Did she have anyone she considered an enemy?"

"No. Girls fight with each other all the time. But it's over nonsense. They make up right away."

I didn't know it at the time, but I would go on to investigate my share of cases where nonsensical disputes led to an autopsy.

"Any adults you can recall acting suspiciously? Looking at her in a leering manner?"

Mr. Mercury said, "She wasn't, was she?"

"No. We have no evidence anything sexual occurred at this point."

"Thank God."

"What about any boyfriends?"

The mother said, "She had one, but they broke up about two weeks ago."

Stone pounced. "What's his name?"

"Dominic Barrow."

"You know his address?"

Mr. Mercury said, "You think it could be him?"

"We don't know anything at this point."

The mother said, "He's a nice boy. I thought they made a cute couple. He lives just a block away."

"Where?"

"On Ravine Drive."

"What was the reason for the breakup?"

"Mary didn't want to be tied down. She was only sixteen. I agreed with her."

"How did the boyfriend take it?"

"Dom was hurt. He came by to try to change her mind, even bringing her flowers. I felt bad for him. He's a good boy."

"Do you think he could have been so upset that he lost control?"

"Oh no. He's harmless."

"What about her close girlfriends? What are their names?"

"Lucy Hart and Denise Wilson."

"How about any girls she didn't like? Anyone she made a negative remark about?"

"I can't think of any offhand. Mary was well liked and had many friends."

"Did she participate in any school or outside activities, cheer-leading or dance? Anything like that?"

"She quit the cheering squad a couple of weeks ago, right after school started. She liked playing tennis and taking dance classes. But nothing serious."

"Why'd she stop being a cheerleader?"

"She said it was too cliquey. Mary was a mature girl for her age, and she felt it was childish."

We finished up with the Mercurys and got back in the car. As soon as I backed out of the driveway, Stone said,

"What do you wanna bet it's the boyfriend?"

"They broke up two weeks ago. Most kids get crushed and get over it in a week."

"You just said the keyword: most. Most people don't strangle others to death."

"We'll check him out. You want to talk to the girlfriends first, right?"

"Nah, let's start with the Barrow kid."

"We might be able to learn something we can use with Barrow if we talk to her friends first."

"We're dealing with teenagers. The kid tries to hide some-thing, I'll smell it."

Chapter Five

Debra was watching the eleven o'clock news when I came in. I gave her a kiss, but she was her usual cold self when I came home late.

"Sorry. It was rough day."

"It was just on the news. Terrible. I can't believe it."

"Yeah, seeing the poor girl like that . . . she was on the ground, with leaves on her. Oh, man."

"Her parents must be devastated."

"You're telling me. We had to notify and then interview them. It was difficult, to say the least."

"I'm sorry."

"It's okay, it's part of the job."

"Did you eat?"

"I got a hero from Mike's Subs."

"I made you prime rib. It's probably like rubber now."

"Why? I told you I was going to be late."

"You said you'd be a little late. Not six hours late. You should've called."

"Sorry, got caught up."

"I know your job is important, but so am I."

"You are. I mean, the kid was just sixteen. It got to me, and I just zoned out."

"I understand, but you can't let it take over your life, our life."

"You're right. I won't let it."

"You better not."

"I'll find a middle ground somewhere. I can't do what I'm doing, but there's no way I'm turning into someone like Stone either. The way he was talking to the parents was almost rude. I wouldn't talk to someone like that if they'd lost a *pet*."

"Then it's the right time for him to retire."

"He's got some great instincts, but man, he's gotten desensitized."

"You better not become like him."

"I won't, and if I do, you better let me know."

"You know I will."

"Yeah, I sure do."

"You think it was a pedophile who did it?"

"No. It doesn't seem like she was sexually assaulted, but we'll know for sure soon. Tomorrow is the autopsy."

"Oh God. What a thing to have to watch."

.

"I know. I'm dreading it already."

"I don't know how you can attend something like that and not let it affect you."

"You get used to it."

"Exactly my point."

"Don't worry. I'm only going to observe ones that are important, and this one is."

IT WAS a typical October morning for New Jersey. It was gray, windy, and chilly. The sweater under my sports jacket kept me warm until I stepped into the autopsy suite. This was the fourth one for me. The three others I attended, while training for homicide, were of people who lived on the edge and showed it.

Seeing the blond, sixteen-year-old on the stainless-steel table gave me a shiver no parka could defend against. The fact she was naked pissed me off. I knew it was necessary, but it felt disrespectful. Her face was so innocent it made me tremble. I didn't know where to look.

I kept my eyes on her neck as Dr. Richter spoke into a microphone hanging over the body. Mary Mercury was officially a statistic. He examined her neck, using tweezers to remove two fibers from the bruise. He said they looked to be made of jute.

He pushed her hair up, looking closely for bruises and abrasions. He scrapped under her fingernails, placing whatever was found in another bag for analysis. Starting at her toes, Richter worked his way up her legs, looked for any irregularities. He took a picture of a bruise on her right knee. It looked a couple of days old to me and harmless but you never knew.

Looking away when he moved toward her private parts, I prayed that Mary wasn't violated. I exhaled when he said there didn't appear to be any abrasions. Looking for traces of semen, he inserted a long Q-tip and bagged the swab.

Richter took a magnifier and combed over the front and sides of the body. He flipped her over and examined the back. When he reached for his scalpel, I looked at Stone and threw a thumb toward the exit. It was time to go. We both believed the organs wouldn't tell us anything. The stomach was the only useful possibility; it could help narrow down the time of death.

BACK IN THE OFFICE, I had an idea. There was a bit of time before Richter would issue the preliminary autopsy report, and I hated to waste time. I said, "Why don't we head over to Middletown South?"

Stone said, "Eh, let's either eliminate the parents or focus on them."

"I put a call into the construction firm. They said he was working. I'm just trying to get a confirmation he was on the three p.m. bus. I asked the sarge to send someone to the Lincroft bus stop today and ask the passengers if he was on it yesterday."

"Good."

"What do you say about going to the school? Maybe there is something in their records about an altercation Mary was involved in."

"Wouldn't they have called the parents about something like that?"

"You never know. Look, at worst, we could find out if she had any friends or activities that she would have shielded from her parents."

The phone of Stone's desk rang. I knew it was Sergeant Gesso. He hung up and stood.

"If you want to go, go ahead. Gesso wants to see me. Said the kid's uncle is making noise."

It was a surprising offer. I wasn't sure if Stone had confidence in me or wanted me get experience running down a lead he felt was a waste of time. Either way, there was no way I could sit on my hands while a killer was on the loose. I swiped the car keys off my desk as he left the office, "See you later."

Chapter Six

Middletown had two high schools, North and South. Bitter sports rivals, there was a belief South was a better school. It might have been true as we seemed to respond to more incidents at the North campus.

The South school was on an access road tucked off Nutswamp Road. It was an ugly building that was built decades ago. The school's blue colors hung over a bank of drab doors.

The principal was Michael Diller. A fifty-something, balding man with a paunch, he was guarded showing me into his office. A group of students were running around the track out the window behind his desk.

"We were shocked to learn about Mary Mercury. We're having a staff meeting this afternoon to explore ways to make sure our students are safe."

I wanted to tell him to start with locking the doors to the school. "We have materials you may find useful. You can get them by calling the traffic and safety department."

"Thank you."

"I'd like to find out whatever you know about Mary Mercury."

"She was an outstanding student. A very nice young lady. She was a member of the cheerleading squad until recently."

"Do you know why she quit?"

"I understand she lost interest."

"Are you sure it wasn't anything else?"

"I don't believe so. Mrs. Meghan, she's the coach, told me Mary had moved on. It's quite common. Students are anxious to be a part of something, and then suddenly, they go cold on the idea."

"Was Mary involved in any altercations, say, over the last year or so?"

"I don't believe so."

"I'd like you check the records."

"Certainly." He picked up the phone and made the request.

"Who would know who her closest friends were?"

"I'd imagine her teachers would know who she hung around with. I can poll them if you like."

"Yes, that would be helpful. I have a couple of names, but I want to be sure we talk to as many people as possible who knew her."

A quick knock sounded, and the door opened. "Here's the file you wanted, Mr. Diller."

"Thank you."

Diller thumbed through the skinny folder. "I didn't think she was involved in any fights. As I said, she was a nice young lady. I just can't understand who could have done something like this. The student body is scared."

"We'll catch whoever is responsible. You can count of that." I stood and held out my business card. "Call me with the names and contact information of her friends."

STONE WAS on the phone when I got back to the office. He hung up, saying, "Richter is going to send over the autopsy report."

"Great."

He smiled. "Find anything at the school?"

"No, but I'm getting a handle on all her friends."

"Okay."

The fax machine started up. I pulled the first sheet to come out. It was warm. "Here we go."

I gave it to Stone as the machine spit out another piece.

"Time of death estimated to be between two and four p.m. That puts it right after the kid got out of school. Cause of death was strangulation using a rope ligature. Well, at least it wasn't painful."

"Maybe not physically, but the kid had to be scared out of her mind."

"You signed up for homicide. Check your emotions at the door."

In this job you had to shut it down or you wouldn't survive, but if doing it turned me into someone without feelings, I'd have to rethink my career path. "I'm not emotional, it's reality."

"Whatever. Look, let's get to work. City hall is about to crawl up our asses."

"What do you want to do next?"

"Talk to the boyfriend."

THE BARROWS LIVED at the end of Ravine Road, one street from the Mercury home. It was also a block closer to the park. We pulled in front of the single-story home. The lawn was covered in leaves.

Stone rang the bell and Edith Barrow answered the door. She did a double take when she saw me. I was ready for her to say that I looked like George Clooney. Edith was wearing jeans, a sweatshirt, and a frown. I showed her my badge asking to see her son, and we settled into a living room just off the foyer. She said, "Let me get Dominick."

Her son was a minor, and we couldn't question him without a parent or attorney present.

Mother and son came into the room. Dominick was a tall, muscular kid with wavy black hair. He looked at his sneakers as we introduced ourselves.

Stone said, "Sit down, Dom. We have a couple of questions about Mary Mercury."

His face darkened as he collapsed onto the couch. His mother sat next to him and patted his leg.

"It's important that you answer our questions honestly and to the best of your recollection. Lying to a law enforcement officer could lead to obstruction of justice charges. Do you understand that?"

What Stone said wasn't exactly true, but it was a good tactic to deploy. I tucked the strategy away.

Barrow nodded.

"Did you strangle Mary Mercury?"

I almost fell off the sofa. Stone was trying to surprise the kid, throw him off.

"That's crazy. Mom!"

Edith had barely recovered. "I don't know what's going on here, but I don't like what you're doing. My son had nothing to do with Mary's, uh, what happened to her."

"I'm sorry to offend you, ma'am, but your son is the one who should answer the question."

"No. I had nothing to do with it. I loved Mary."

"You two were going steady, right?"

"Yeah."

"When did it end?"

"Thirteen days ago."

"She broke it off?"

"Yeah."

"Why?"

"She said she didn't want to be tied down, that she was too young."

"How did that make you feel?"

"I was upset."

"Angry?"

"No. I wasn't like, mad or anything. More like depressed, you know."

"Where were you the day she was murdered?"

"I went to school and came home."

"What did you do when you came home?"

"Did some homework and played a video game."

"Was anyone home with you?"

"No. My mom works on Tuesdays."

"Dominick is right. I work the Friday through Tuesday shift at Bayshore Hospital."

"What game were you playing?"

"*Mortal Combat.*"

"Who do you think could have done this to Mary?"

"I don't know. It's crazy. Like, who would want to hurt her. She was"—his lip quivered—"the best."

"Did she argue with anyone recently?"

"No. She was kind to everyone. Some people thought she was a phony, but that was really her."

"Was anyone jealous of her?"

"I guess so. I heard a couple of girls call her Mother Mary."

Chapter Seven

We left the Barrow house with a new name: Judy Forlow. The girl was another friend of Mary's, one who Barrow claimed she was closest to.

"You were a little rough on the kid."

"You got good instincts, Luca, but you're too soft. We're not out here to make friends. Our job is to nail the killer and quick."

It was hard to ignore the success that Stone had piled up. He had been a member of a multi-agency task force that involved the FBI and received a commendation for his work there. I knew he was good, but I thought there was a way to close cases without his wrecking-ball approach.

"I guess we should start with Mary's girlfriends."

"Yeah, you got the addresses with you?"

"Yep. I even called the ones Mrs. Mercury told us about, told them to stick around the house because we'd need to talk to them." I took my notebook out.

"Good. You know, you impress me sometimes."

Sometimes? "Thanks. Lucy Hart lives on the other side of Middletown-Lincroft Road on Blue Jay Court. It's only five minutes away."

The Harts lived on a small street. The developer had done almost nothing to differentiate the homes he put up. Each one's front had red bricks going up halfway, topped with white siding.

A petite woman, with her hair pulled back, opened the door. I held my badge up. "Mrs. Hart?"

"Yes. But I'm no longer married. Just haven't gotten around to changing my name back."

We entered a hallway, stepping around a collection of shoes. She led us into a kitchen. My mom would have gotten nervous with how much stuff was sitting on the counters.

"Take a seat. I'll get Lucy." She opened the door to the backyard. Her daughter was playing with a dog. It was a cute little thing.

Between her willow-thin frame and ghostly complexion, Lucy Hart looked malnourished. Mrs. Hart said,

"Lucy, these detectives would like to talk to you about Mary."

"Sure. I really miss her."

I said, "We're sorry for your loss."

"I still can't believe it."

Stone said, "Who do you think did it?"

"I don't know. Mary was nice to everybody even if they were mean to her."

"Who was mean to her?"

"Not, like, real mean, you know, but you could tell, you know."

"No, I don't know. Tell me what you mean."

"Sometimes, people, they say one thing, but you know they don't mean it, right?"

Stone sighed. "Just tell me the names of the people who were mean or whatever you meant by it."

"Some of the girls on the cheering squad."

"I don't have all day, kiddo. Names, I need names."

"Mary never said who. She just mentioned that she felt like an outsider."

Before Stone could say anything, I said, "Did she get into an argument with any of them?"

"I don't think so. She never said anything."

Stone said, "What about her boyfriend, Dominick Barrow?"

"I mean, Mary only was seeing him for a short time. It's not nice to say, but I think she went with him 'cause she was bored."

"He must have taken the breakup badly."

It was a leading question that would've gotten tossed in any supervised setting.

"I guess so."

"Either he did or didn't. Which one is it?"

"Dom is kind of a, I don't know how to say it, but he's, like, off a tiny bit. Not all the time, but sometimes he says things or does things that are weird."

"Give me an example."

"Last year, on the Fourth of July, he was taking frogs and taping firecrackers to them. It was gross. I couldn't look at it."

"Where did he do that?"

"We were all at Denise's house for a barbecue, and he was doing it in the street."

"What else?"

"Oh yeah, he used to talk about hanging out in the cemetery. It was creepy."

"What did he do there?"

"I think him and Kenny used to go smoke there."

"Cigarettes or something else?"

"I don't know."

"Who's Kenny?"

"Kenny Spencer. He goes to North; I don't know him well, but he's a troublemaker."

We couldn't get anything more out of Lucy and got back in the car. When I started the car up, Stone said, "I'm feeling it's the Barrow kid."

"What makes you say that?"

"He's got a violent streak."

"Because he blew up a frog?"

"Yeah, and who hangs out in the cemetery?"

"Sounds like a normal teenage boy to me."

"We'll see."

The radio in the car crackled. It was Sergeant Gesso.

"Hey, boys, how you making out?"

Stone said, "Talking to more teenagers than I'd like to."

"Good thing you didn't become a father, then."

It made me think of my own reluctance to have a child. Debra had started to mention it more regularly, but I kept putting it off. I wanted to concentrate on my career, but the longer I worked in law enforcement, the more concerned I became about bringing a kid into such a crazy world.

My mother was always there for me, somehow guiding me through all life's pitfalls. I just didn't know if I could do that with my own child. I remembered when I was only fourteen, and two kids on the block had gotten killed trying to run across the highway as some sort of game. I told my mom that I was afraid of something like that happening to my kid, or maybe they'd get on drugs or become a criminal. She said I shouldn't worry about it, that if I brought up my kids the way I knew to, it would be all right.

I adored my mother and didn't challenge it, but even at fourteen, it sounded like bullshit. But as I got older, I realized it was a way of saying to do what you think was right. It made sense, but I wasn't ready to put it to the test.

Stone chuckled. "You're probably right."

"Is Luca with you?"

"Yes, sir. I'm driving."

"You asked me to check on the bus that Mr. Mercury said he was on. I sent a car down to the Academy bus stop in Lincroft. None of the regulars on the three p.m. out of Port Authority said he was on it. In fact, one guy said he took the one p.m. out on Tuesday, and he said Mercury was on it with him."

"Thanks, sir."

"Be safe, guys."

Stone said, "Holy shit. Wasn't it you that was busting my balls for going too hard on the parents?"

He was right. "I can't believe it. Why would he lie to us?"

Chapter Eight

We waited until five p.m. to make sure Mr. Mercury was home from work. I had my doubts whether he killed his daughter, but the fact was, victims were often killed by someone close. I didn't want to think about it, but though the doctor claimed there were no signs of sexual abuse, the only thing that could explain it was some kind of abuse.

It was a sick scenario: Mary being abused by her father. She wanted it to stop and had threatened to reveal it. To keep her quiet, Mercury killed her. Just thinking about it threw a spray of bile against the rear of my throat.

We walked up to the door in the dark. Daylight savings time made no sense to me. I was about to press the bell when I heard a male voice yelling. I looked at Stone and put an ear against the door. I couldn't make out what the argument was about.

I hit the bell and pounded the door with a palm. The guy we came to see opened the door. His face was flushed. He stared at us for a moment, then said, "You have news for us?"

It was the right thing to say. Stone said, "No, but we'd like to talk. Can we come in?"

"Uh, sure."

We stepped in. Mrs. Mercury poked her head into the foyer. Her face crumpled when she saw us. It looked like she'd been crying. She said, "Is everything all right?"

I said, "Yes. We're sorry to disturb you, ma'am, but we have a couple of questions for your husband. It shouldn't take long."

She came forward and led the way to the living room. Photo albums were spread on the floor, and the coffee table held a stack of loose photos.

"Sorry, we're getting things ready for the, the wake."

Her husband said, "When is our daughter going to be released to us?"

I said, "I believe within a day. They're just waiting on the lab results to be sure they have everything."

Mrs. Mercury sniffled, and her husband reached for her hand. "This has been painful enough."

"We realize that and we're sorry. It won't be long."

"What did you want to ask?"

Stone said, "Mr. Mercury, we asked you when you had gotten home the day we found your daughter. I believe you said that you took the three p.m. bus out of Port Authority."

"Yeah, that's right."

"And you got off at Lincroft?"

"Yes."

"What time did it arrive?"

"I don't know, about four. Why?"

"Are you sure you were on that bus?"

"Of course I was. You saw me right after I got off. I came straight home."

"That's interesting because no one remembers you being on it."

"You checked on me? That's crazy. What the hell is going on here?"

"That's exactly what I want to know. You weren't on the bus

you said you were. In fact, someone said they saw you on the one p.m. out of the city."

His wife's hands were shaking. I felt bad for the woman. "That's not right. I was on the three p.m."

"Not according to the witnesses."

"Look, just what are you trying to say?"

"We need to establish alibis for everyone connected to the case. Right now, you have a two-hour window that needs explaining."

"Bullshit. I was on the bus I said I was. Whoever you asked don't know what they're talking about."

"Three different witnesses were unable to confirm your presence on the three p.m., and another put you on an earlier one."

"Well, they're wrong."

Mrs. Mercury started sobbing. "Leave him alone. He didn't do anything. He'd never harm Mary."

Her husband stood. "I think it's time you leave."

Driving back to the station, Stone said, "He's hiding something."

"Maybe we should double check. Maybe he's telling the truth, and the people mixed up the dates."

"Go ahead and do that. We know eyewitnesses aren't reliable but four of them making a mistake? Seems highly unlikely. I'm going to dig into this guy."

Stone was right. People confused things all the time, even two could but not four. I was going to focus on the earlier bus. If we could get another person or two confirming Mr. Mercury was on the 1 p.m. run, he'd have to change his story.

DEBRA WAS DOING a jigsaw puzzle when I came through the door. She said, "Home early?"

"Not really, it's almost seven."

"For you? Even when you're not on a case, you don't get home before eight."

"Well, I'm on a case, and I'm home before seven. I'm starving. What's for dinner?"

"I didn't expect you. You want to go out?"

"Not really. You wanna order Chinese?"

"Okay."

I grabbed a beer and Golden Dragon's takeout menu. After I phoned in the order, Linda said, "What's going on with the girl's murder? They had her uncle on the news saying the police had to do more to catch the killer."

"More? We're doing all we can. It's early. You know we're looking at her father."

"Her father? Don't tell me he did it."

"I'm not saying he did, but his alibi don't hold water."

"I saw the parents; they were on yesterday. I can't imagine it was him. He was heartbroken."

"I'm sure he was, but in a lot of homicides, it's a family member, and most of the time the killer is male and the victim is female."

"They seem pretty normal to me."

"Maybe, but here's another interesting fact. Did you know that when a family member kills another, they usually don't use a gun?"

"Really? So you think it was him?"

"I don't know, but Stone thinks it's a possibility."

Chapter Nine

I was balancing the *Post* and a coffee opening the door to our office when a cute officer came up. She had a phone message in her hand. She had just started and had the goods. Even the uniform couldn't hide her curves.

She held out the message. "This guy just called."

"Damn, I thought you were going to give me your phone number."

She lit up the hall with her smile.

"So how are you doing?"

"Bored, to be honest. I can't wait to go out on patrol."

"Why don't we get a drink one night? I can fill you in on the whos whats and wheres."

She gave me another ten-thousand-watt smile and turned around.

I watched her go down the hallway. Well, her ass anyway. She was exaggerating the sway and shake. It provoked the desired response in me. She was flirting and I was intrigued.

Thinking of ways to get to know her better, I set the paper and coffee down and took my jacket off. Looking at the pink slip she'd given me, thoughts of getting between the sheets with her vanished.

Mr. Mercury had called. I sat down. Should I wait for Stone to speak with him? Why'd he call me? He knew I was the junior detective. Did he think it would be easier getting one over on me?

People miscalculated all the time. He didn't strike me as someone who thought he was smarter than everyone else, but he had fed us what seemed to be a lie on his whereabouts.

I looked at the message. The callback number had a 212 area code. Manhattan. He was working? I checked the time. It was quarter to eight. Stone always strolled in just before nine.

There was no way I could wait an hour and change to find out what Mercury wanted. I picked up the phone and dialed the number. Bombarded with noise from the receiver being left off the hook, I waited for them to locate Mercury.

"Hello?"

"Mr. Mercury, this is Detective Luca. You called this morning?"

"Yes, yes. Look, about the whole bus business thing. Look, I told you I was on the three o'clock, but I wasn't."

"We know that. Why didn't you say that yesterday?"

"Well, I couldn't because my wife was there." He lowered his voice. "Look, I was with another woman. I took the earlier bus, went to see her, and then I came home."

"You're having an affair?"

"Yeah."

Based on my record of chasing women, I was in no position to judge him. "I see."

"It's like God punished me with what happened to Mary."

It was another thing I didn't believe in. God wasn't keeping a scorecard and meting out justice as he saw fit. If he did, there'd be no need for homicide detectives. "Where were you doing this?"

"At her apartment. She lives in Hazlet, in back of the Red Oak Diner."

"What's her name and address?"

"Oh, come on. I don't want my wife to know. It'll kill her, especially with what happened."

"I understand. I'll keep it quiet. Who is she?"

"I don't want to drag her into this."

"You have no choice. You lied to us. Now, we need to verify everything."

"Are you sure my wife won't find out?"

"If she does, it won't come from me. I promise you the information will remain confidential."

"All right. Her name is Barbara Cowan. She lives at 37 Meadow Drive, in Hazlet."

"What's her phone number?"

Before he gave it to me, he said, "Can you give me a minute to call her."

"You got it. She home now?"

"Yeah, she works nights."

"Okay. It's none of my business, but how come you went into work today?"

"I came in to pick up my check. I would've been out of here already, but I was waiting for you to call."

After hanging up, I thought about how circumstances upended the plans people made. Here was a guy cheating on his wife, who could never have imagined how his affair would come to light. It was a reminder I needed to take into account my own dalliances. What was I thinking when I interacted with the new officer?

The last thing I wanted to do was hurt Debra. It had been a while since I had strayed, and maybe seeing this guy get jammed up was what I needed. It was true that women were always flirting with me, but instead of letting it feed my ego, I needed to tone it down and keep it light.

I picked up the phone and dialed. A female, someone with a smoker's voice answered. "Hello."

"Is this Barbara Cowan?"

"Yes, is this the police?"

Mercury had gotten through. "I'm Detective Luca. Were you with Mr. Mercury on October 10 between the hours of two and four p.m.?"

"Yes. He came over that afternoon."

"I have to warn you that if you're covering for him, you're committing obstruction of justice. We'll charge you, and it's punishable by up to eighteen months in jail plus a sizable fine."

It was the same threat Stone had made to Dominick Barrow, but in this case it was true. You couldn't lie to protect someone who could be responsible for a crime.

"No, no. You have to believe me. He was here. He comes over almost every Tuesday."

"Who can back up what you're telling me? Did anyone see him at your place?"

"Oh, I don't know. I told Cheryl, she's my friend, right after I heard what happened to his daughter. I called her right away. I couldn't believe he was just here and then . . ."

"I'm going to need an eyewitness."

"We were inside the whole time Bobby was here."

"You understand I'm going to have to look further into this?"

"I guess so, but can you try and keep it quiet?"

Chapter Ten

Stone came in ten minutes after nine. He looked like he'd had a rough night. He grumbled a good morning.

"Morning. Looks like the kid's father is in the clear."

He fell into his chair. "You talking about Robert Mercury?"

"Yep. Looks like he was stepping out on his wife. He called early this morning. He took the one p.m. bus and went to see a woman named Barbara Cowan over in Hazlet. I spoke with her. Apparently, they've been having an affair for some time."

"Is there anybody who can corroborate it?"

"Neither of them gave me anyone else."

"Make sure you check it out. She could be covering for him."

"Absolutely."

"Get her address and go there. They may have been inside screwing like a couple of lovebirds, but I guarantee you a nosy neighbor or two saw him arrive or leave."

It was a good idea. "I'll check it out."

"Go around the time they're claiming he was there. You should catch whoever was around then."

"That's true. You think I should wait for Tuesday, then?"

"Nah, if you can't clear him now, we'll try Tuesday. If we can move him off the radar, it'll help us focus."

"You got it."

The cute officer stepped into the office with a manila envelope, handing it to Stone.

"This is for you. It's from the ME."

Before he could say thanks, she turned toward me, flashing a wide smile. "So, how are you doing?"

She was sweet. "Busy. You know, with this kid's case."

"It makes you think, doesn't it? Do what you want to do, while you can, right?"

Was that an invitation of some kind? Before I could make a decision on how to respond, Stone cleared his throat.

"Look, I gotta go right now."

"Sure. Bye, bye."

I stared at her ass. Stone said, "You're gonna end up like Mercury if you keep it up."

"What?"

He opened the envelope. "Be careful. Especially at work. My old man told me something that stuck with me all these years and he was right. He said not to shit in your own backyard."

The wisdom of the elders. "It's probably not how Buddha would have said it but it's sound advice."

"Richter sent the autopsy report."

I came around his desk. Stone said, "Death by asphyxiation. She was strangled to death like we all thought. You see this." He pointed to a paragraph. "Anytime there's a fracture of the hyoid bone, it's almost a guarantee."

"And the petechia."

"Not always. I've seen at least two cases where there weren't hemorrhages even though they were choked to death."

They never said that in my classes at John Jay College. "I didn't know that."

"She didn't have any alcohol or foreign substances in her

system. No signs of sexual abuse or activity of any kind. He's confirming a rope was used and the fibers were jute."

"That's a common type of rope."

"He put down a width range of a quarter to half an inch. Time of death didn't change from the prelim."

"What about that bruise on her knee?"

Stone ran a finger down the page and turned to the next sheet. "He doesn't believe it was related but doesn't completely rule it out."

"What about the fingernails? Richter scraped them."

"Just fibers of jute and one fiber from a black nylon fabric."

An image of the kid clawing at the rope flashed through my mind. "Anything we can go on?"

"Outside of officially ruling out some sort of sexual motivation, there's nothing the good doctor told me I didn't know after seeing the body."

"And no drinking or drugs."

"We got to figure this one out on our own. Let's go see the victim's other girlfriends."

DENISE WILSON WAS the other name Mary's mother had given us. She was tall, like her mother, and hunched her shoulders in an attempt at masking her height. Mrs. Wilson cleared the kitchen table of text books and papers and we took seats. The room was tight and dark. I tamped down a flare of claustrophobia.

Stone said, "We're trying to learn as much about Mary as we can. We need to know if there was anyone she may have fought with or if she mentioned being afraid of someone, or threatened in anyway."

"Mary was the sweetest person you could know. I'm not just saying that; she really was."

"Who do you think could have done this?"

"I don't know. Really. I thought a lot about it, but I can't imagine someone doing it."

"It's hard to imagine, but people snap all the time. Is there anyone who acted strange, in any way?"

"I can't think of anyone."

"What about her boyfriend, Dominick Barrow?"

"She wasn't serious about him. It was more like a couple of dates. That's all it was."

"I understand he took it badly when she broke it off."

"Yeah, she told me he kept calling her, wouldn't leave her alone."

"Do you think there's any chance he could have done this?"

"Dominick?"

"Yes."

"He's weird but . . ."

"But what?"

"You know, I just remembered that there was something going around that he killed a cat."

"When was this?"

"Uh, oh yeah. It was right after school started last year."

"Who told you that he killed a cat?"

"I don't know. People were talking about it."

"And what happened?"

"Nothing. It was like, one day it was the thing to talk about, and the next day nobody cared about it."

It sounded like the network news to me.

"How did he kill it?"

"I think he might have stabbed it or something. I don't really remember what they said happened."

Stone pressed for more details, but the kid couldn't produce any. He ended the interview. I went to turn the ignition on when he said, "It's probably going to be Barrow. It looks like he's violent."

"Could be just a rumor. She didn't have any details on it."

"Kid blows up frogs and may have stabbed a cat to death? That *Mortal Combat* video game is filled with violence. There's a pattern and we got to check it out."

Chapter Eleven

I turned onto Route 35. Stone pointed. "Pull over. There's a telephone booth. Call the Barrows, and make sure they're home."

It would take an act of God to change Stone's focus but I had to try. "But we have an appointment to see Judy Forlow."

"So?"

"It might be good to talk to her, get some color. Barrow said she was close to Mary, and no one even mentioned her."

He gave me the look you'd give someone who said he'd seen a spaceship. "Trust me on this, okay?"

Stuffing a quarter into the slot, I hoped no one would answer. One ring. Two. Three. I cut the connection with my finger and waited ten more seconds before hanging up the receiver.

"No one's home."

"Damn it."

"Let's go see this kid. We're close enough."

Forlow lived in a section of Middletown called Belford. Her Cape Cod-styled home was framed by two overgrown oak trees. A woman, I took for her grandmother, turned out to be her mother. She showed us into a small living room, told us to sit, then disappeared. We took chairs facing a fireplace.

Judy Forlow, her mother trailing behind, bounced into the room. She wore a Rock and Roll Hall of Fame T-shirt with a picture of Led Zeppelin and cranberry jeans. We introduced ourselves. She sat saying, "I was wondering if anybody was going to talk to me about Mary."

Stone said, "You were close with her?"

"Yeah, we got along really well. I miss her. Sometimes we'd talk for hours on the phone."

"About what?"

"This and that, you know, girl stuff."

"You talk about Dominick Barrow?"

"Yeah, sometimes, but not a lot."

"You're friends with Dominick as well?"

"Yeah, but not the same, like with Mary."

"But you know him well?"

Stone was leading. Again. "Yeah, well enough."

"Do you think he could have done this to Mary?"

"No. No way. He's not like that."

"He took getting dumped by Mary hard, didn't he?"

"He's a sensitive kid."

"Sensitive? From what we hear, he's violent."

"No, he isn't."

"Didn't he kill a cat?"

"That was an accident."

"How do you know that?"

"He told me it was."

"Whose cat was it?"

"The lady across the street. She's a total witch."

Her mother said, "Judy, that's not nice. I don't want you talking like that."

Judy rolled her eyes. "Okay, already."

"What happened?"

"I don't really know. It was like a year ago, before we got friendly."

"Did Mary tell you anything that now makes you think?"

"Not really. I mean, I remember she said there was this guy. She said he was creepy and that he followed her one time when she was going home from cheering practice."

"When was this?"

"A couple of weeks ago."

"Did this happen again?"

"She never said."

"Did she describe him?"

"Just that he was older."

"How old? Like him?" He pointed to me. "Or a couple of years older than her?"

"She didn't say, but I kinda thought it was like someone around twenty."

"What gave you that impression?"

"I don't know, it just did. Otherwise, she would have said like some ancient guy."

Thanks. I was early thirties, and she thought I was a fossil.

"We've heard that Dominic Barrow got physical with Mary."

I almost fell off the chair. Where was that coming from? Was he holding back information?

"What? Who said that? I never heard anything like that. She would have told me. Definitely."

"Maybe she was embarrassed about it."

"She told me everything. And I mean, everything."

We concluded the interview and got back in the car. I waited until I made a U-turn before asking, "What was all that about the Barrow kid getting physical?"

"Doing a little fishing."

"I don't know about that."

"I do. You got to shake things to get something to drop. Let's go see Barrow."

As I drove past a strip center, Stone said, "You know about five years ago, me and Hartman worked a case where the body was found in a house back there. This guy, he reported his wife missing. It didn't add up to me. Everybody bought his story but me. There was evidence his wife was screwing around, and everyone bought his bullshit that she'd taken off on him."

"What happened?"

"I kept digging into him. Hartman told me I was wasting my time. Even Gesso said to let it go, but I couldn't. My gut was telling me he killed her. I went way back on him. Found out when he was twenty-five that he'd worked as a mason, doing brickwork and laying tile for five years. It was like bingo to me. You see, I remembered going to his house, and he had this new floor that I liked. I said something about it once, and he changed the subject right away."

"Don't tell me she was buried under there."

"You got it. It wasn't easy getting the warrant, but the bastard is serving twenty-five to life."

"That's incredible. What did Hartman say to that?"

"You know, my partner was a good guy, but he was a little too soft at times. If I would've listened to him, the bastard would be laughing at us."

I made a left onto Ravine Drive and parked in front of the Barrow home. Stone pointed across the street. "I want to check out this dead-cat story."

A woman in her late sixties came to the door. Wearing a blue sweater over a housecoat, she was holding a tiny white dog. It got excited when it saw us. We introduced ourselves and I said, "That's a cute dog. What is it?"

Mrs. Amper said, "A teacup Maltese."

I extended my hand. The puppy licked it like it was peanut butter. Stone leaned away as if it was a Pit Bull foaming at the mouth. He said, "Can we get to the questions I have about your neighbor?"

"Sure, come in. It's chilly out there."

We stepped into the foyer, declining an offer to sit. Stone said,

"We understand you had a cat that died while in the care of Dominick Barrow."

"Yes. He denies it, but I know he killed my Gladys."

"Tell us what happened."

"Well, I was going upstate, and my granddaughter was graduating from Cornell—she's a smart one, finished a semester early, she did. But the poor kid is allergic to cats. I needed someone to care of Gladys for a couple of days and asked Betty to take her in."

"Betty Barrow?"

"Yes. She's a nice lady, but that kid of hers. I don't know what went wrong with him."

"Dominick Barrow?"

"Yep."

"So you gave the cat to Mrs. Barrow to watch while you went to see your granddaughter. What happened?"

"Well, I get home and first thing I did was go to see my Gladys. As soon as Betty opened the door, I knew something was wrong. She said Gladys had died earlier that day. I was in shock. I thought she was kidding but it was true. She took me in the garage, and there she was, lying in her bed. She looked so sad. I picked her up hoping she'd be okay but . . ."

"What did she say happened to your cat?"

"Nothing, that she just died. I didn't believe it and took her straight to the vet. Dr. Spencer said Gladys had died from asphyxiation. Said someone had tied something around her neck and choked my poor baby to death."

Stone glanced at me and said, "Did you confront Mrs. Barrow about it?"

"Of course I did. She said nothing happened, but I pushed her to ask her son about it. She called Dominick, and he lied right to my face, said he didn't do anything. I knew he was lying and told Betty right in front of him. Well, she must've gone hard on him 'cause the next day she called to say that she'd gone grocery shopping and left Gladys with Dominick. She said he'd put the cat in the bathroom because he was afraid she'd get lost outside. He told his mother he found her hanging from the doorknob, that Gladys had tried to get out and hung herself."

"Did you ask the vet about the possibility?"

"He said he'd have to do an autopsy to confirm, but I'd already had her cremated."

Chapter Twelve

Stone didn't say anything as he marched across the street. Mrs. Barrow opened the door wearing an apron. Her face dropped so fast, I thought it'd slide off her skull.

"It's not a good time. I'm in the middle of preparing dinner."

"We need to talk to you and your son."

"How about tomorrow?"

"That's not going to work. I have questions needing answering. Now."

Mrs. Barrow backed into the foyer. "Okay."

We followed her into the kitchen. Dominick was at the table doing homework. He looked up and went back to writing.

"Dominick, the detectives have more questions for you about Mary."

"Okay."

We sat across from him and I studied the kid's face. He had a look of concern, but people always got nervous when the police showed up.

I said, "Have you given more thought as to who could have done it?"

"Yeah, I racked my brain but can't come up with anyone. I

mean, Judy said something about a guy following Mary after school but that's all I know."

"When did she tell you that?"

"A little while ago, she called."

Stone said, "You realize we'll find out the truth, don't you?"

"I guess so."

"No, I know so. Now, I understand you like to kill animals."

"No I don't."

"Didn't you blow up frogs on the Fourth of July."

"That was nothing. We were just fooling around."

Mrs. Barrow looked like she'd seen a severed head.

"What about the cat?"

"The cat?"

"Don't play dumb with me. Mrs. Amper believes you strangled her cat."

"I didn't. I swear. It was an accident."

"Tell me what happened."

"I didn't do anything. There's nothing to say. Mom went shopping and I was here. It was nice out so I had the slider open. I didn't want the cat to run away so I put it in the bathroom. When I went to get her, she was hanging from her collar on the doorknob. It freaked me out."

"Show me where this happened?"

We went to a bathroom. A shower curtain obscured the back wall. Stone grabbed the lever-type door handle.

"You're telling me the cat jumped up and got caught on this?"

"Yeah."

He held the lever down. "And when you came in, the cat was still on the handle?"

"Yes."

"It would seem to me that it would have slid off. Are you sure?"

"No, it was still on. The collar was wrapped on this part." Barrow touched the stem of the handle.

"That seems highly unlikely."

"I don't care if you believe me or not. That's what happened."

I knew cats could jump, but would they need a running start to get that high? I counted the white tiles that made up the floor. From the door to the tub there were ten. It looked like more than enough.

I grabbed the lever. Trying to envision a cat getting caught up on it, Stone said, "You didn't like the cat, did you?"

"I don't like any cats, but I didn't do anything to hers."

"You choked the cat to death. Didn't you?"

"No! Mom, tell them I didn't do anything."

"My son has denied killing the cat. It was an accident. It's unfortunate, but the cat hung itself."

WHILE DRIVING to check on Robert Mercury's alibi, I went over the Barrow interview. I didn't know what to make of the cat story. The kid seemed to be the slightest bit off. But when he was accused by Stone, he didn't waver and never averted his eyes.

Unless his mother was covering up, there were no known witnesses. I tried to come up with a way to determine if it was an accident or not. If he tried to choke it with his hands, the cat would have gone wild. Its claws would have scratched, if not shredded, Barrow's arms.

It could be something to look into, but the odds were the kid knew it and would have used a rope to hang it. I pulled into a space in front of Cowan's place thinking it was possible that Barrow told a friend about it. Maybe someone he was trying to impress or someone who'd done evil themselves.

Cowan's door was one of four in the brick building. As I walked up to her apartment, the curtains in the next apartment were pulled aside, and a woman's face peeked out. I found the busy-body.

I thought about going straight to the snoopy lady but thought I should speak with Cowan first. Besides, I was curious to see what the woman Mercury was risking his marriage for looked like.

When Barbara Cowan opened the door, I kind of figured where Mercury was coming from. Though she was plain looking, Cowan was ten years younger and had a chest that was hard to keep your eyes off.

I flashed my badge. "We spoke on the phone."

"Come in."

"I just have a couple of questions, for the record."

"Okay. You know you look like George Clooney."

I nodded. "Was Robert Mercury here on October tenth?"

"Yes. It was Tuesday. I remember."

"What time did he get here?"

"A little after two o'clock."

"And he left when?"

"Just about four."

An afternoon quickie. "That was a fast visit."

"He had to stay longer at work that day. Usually, he gets here by one."

"Where did he park?"

"Right out front."

"All right, Miss Cowan. I'll be in touch if I need anything further."

I turned to go, and she put her hand on my arm. Was she about to make a pass at me?

"Bobby didn't do it. He loved his daughter. He's a good person. Please believe me, it wasn't him."

"We have to check everything out."

I pressed the neighbor's bell. The chime was still ringing when a woman in her seventies opened the door.

"Detective Luca, Middletown Police. I'd like to ask you a question or two."

"Nice to meet you, I'm Madeline White. You know, I figured you were the law."

"Well, I'm glad you have a sharp eye, ma'am. I'm interested in whatever you may have seen on Tuesday, October tenth."

"I saw you went to Barbara's. So you must know she had her regular playdate with her boyfriend."

"You saw a man go to her apartment on Tuesday, October tenth?"

"Yes, he was later than usual though. They usually have their rendezvous around one. I remember it was right after the mailman came."

I liked this lady. She told it straight and didn't care that anyone knew she was keeping her eye on you. "You seem confident about what you saw. Were you looking out the window all day?"

"I'm an old lady but my hearing? I can hear a pin drop, they say. Anytime a car comes into the lot, I check to see who it is. Started doing it about eight months ago, right after we had two break-ins. If I see something out of place, I call it in. Last month, these teenagers were checking to see what cars were unlocked. I flicked the lights on and off and they ran. Called 911 anyway."

"That's good. I wish more people were as attentive as you are. And by the way, you're not old. You can't be a day over sixty, right?"

She laughed. I said goodbye, making a mental note to ask Gesso to increase patrols in the area.

Chapter Thirteen

I pulled out of the parking lot. As soon as the station fell from view, Stone said, "Put the lights on."

"Now? You sure?"

"Yep."

It seemed unnecessary. Every officer knew flashing lights scared the hell out of drivers, freezing them or causing them to move haphazardly. Discretion was allowed, but there were guidelines, and reprimands were regularly handed out.

Stone was pushing it because it appeared we had a witness. We had posted an officer at the park between the hours of two and four p.m. asking for information. People were creatures of habit. If they went for a walk or took the dog to the park, they usually did it at the same time of day.

After three days, a woman came forward, saying she had seen something. Her name was Wendy O'Rourke. She was waiting at the park. I put the heat up a notch as we approached Poricy Park, hoping to absorb it before we got out of the car.

Stepping out of the car, I zipped up my jacket. The potential witness was jogging in place. She looked about forty. We introduced ourselves. I took out my notebook.

Stone said, "We understand you might have seen something on Tuesday afternoon."

"Yes, that's what I was telling the other officer."

She was wearing running pants and a Juicy Couture sweatshirt. "Okay, Miss O'Rourke, tell me, what did you see?"

"I saw a kid. Well, not really a kid—"

"Approximately, how old?"

"Tough to say. I didn't see his face, more like his back with some of the side of his face. I think he could be, say, late teens to maybe thirty?"

I made notes as Stone continued. "What about his hair color and build?"

"Dark hair, medium sized."

"What was he wearing?"

"Jeans and one of those Members Only jackets."

"Color?"

"Black."

"What time was this?"

"About three, three fifteen or so."

"Where did you see this kid?"

"I'm not sure it was a kid though. He was over there." She pointed to a spot off the trail.

"Let's walk over there."

She stopped about fifty yards into the park. "I was running along here, and I saw him out of the corner of my eye. See the tree there with the branches making a Y? He was just to the right of it, walking into the woods."

"Did he see you?"

"I don't know. He could have heard me running. But it's not like I was staring at him."

"Why did you wait until today to say something?"

"I didn't put two and two together until I saw the policeman today."

"But don't you come here every day?"

"No. I vary my routine. I run five miles a day. If I took the same route I'd die of boredom."

"Did you see anyone else in the park?"

"Some lady was walking her dog, kind of in the back, where the path turns."

We went to the place she saw the woman walking her dog. Stone said, "Is this woman someone you've seen before?"

"Uhm. Maybe. I don't pay much attention when I'm jogging." She patted the sweater's pocket. "I listen to my Walkman and kind of get into a zone."

What she was saying made sense. I ran for a while, a short one. It was a mind game. If I distracted myself, I could do two miles. If I couldn't, I'd be out of breath after a couple of blocks.

I said, "What kind of a dog was it?"

"A poodle. It was black, not one of those small ones. It was regular sized with a puffy head."

"How old was the owner?"

"Around sixty."

"Were there any cars in the lot that day?"

"You know, I don't think so."

The poodle owner lived in the area.

Stone said, "Give us your contact information. We may have more questions or ask you to look at a photo of someone, see if you recognize him as the kid you saw."

I wrote down the information, wondering who Stone was referring to.

ANOTHER CALL to the hotline was patched through to my desk. "Detective Luca. How can I help you?"

"I saw the news, you wanted to talk to anyone who had a black poodle."

"Do you live near Poricy Park?"

"No, I live off Kings Highway."

"Do you walk your dog in Poricy Park?"

"No, it's too far away."

"We're looking for poodle owners who were walking their dogs in Poricy on October tenth."

"Why didn't they say that, then?"

"I'm sorry the message wasn't clear, ma'am. But thank you for calling."

They did. I saw the news play our request for help. It was clear and featured the park in the background. People just don't listen. The public is often helpful, which is why we put up with crackpots calling the hotlines. In this case, this lady was the fourth one who thought we were interested in poodles.

Stone said, "And they say men have selective hearing."

"Only when the wife is talking."

The phone rang again. "Detective Luca."

"Uh, hi. I saw the news, and I think it was me and Daisy at the park."

I snapped my fingers and gave Stone a thumbs-up. "Thank you for calling, ma'am. Can I have your name?"

"Clara Cox."

"Were you at Poricy Park on Tuesday, October tenth?"

"Yes, I took Daisy for a walk."

"What time was that?"

"Uhmm. Around three. I'm not sure exactly because we walked there, and on the way, one of my neighbors, Mrs. Johnson, had just come home, and we started talking for a while."

"Is it possible for you to meet us at Poricy Park?"

"When?"

"As soon as possible. We can pick you up if you'd like."

"No, I'll drive over. Can you give me fifteen minutes?"

"See you then. And thanks again for coming forward."

"Looks like we found the poodle lady. She's on her way to the park now."

Chapter Fourteen

A car pulled into Poricy Park's lot. A female in her forties got out. The woman approached our car. I opened the window.

"Can I help you?"

"I'm supposed to meet a detective here. I think his name was Luca."

"I'm sorry, I'm Detective Luca. I didn't recognize you."

Scrambling out of the car, I questioned the recall of Wendy O'Rourke, the jogger we'd spoken to.

"Thank you for meeting us on such a short notice, but this case is an important one."

"I feel terrible about what happened to that girl."

Stone said, "You were walking your dog that afternoon?"

"Yes, I don't come here often because she gets too dirty, but once a week or so, I take Daisy here."

"What time was that?"

"I was telling Officer Luca that it was around three o'clock."

"How long were you here?"

"Maybe fifteen to twenty minutes."

"Was there anyone else in the park during that time?"

"Yes, a woman, about my age, was running, and a man was walking in the woods."

"Can you describe the man?"

"I didn't see the front of him. He was walking away from me."

"How do you know it was a man and not, say, a teenager?"

"I didn't mean to say it was a man, man.

"Show us where you were when you saw him and where he was."

We stopped at a point where the path turned to the left. "I was about here; Daisy was sniffing around for a place for her to do her business and I saw him over there." She pointed into the woods. I was certain whoever she saw was headed in the direction of the railroad tracks.

"What was he wearing?"

"Looked like dungarees and a dark-colored jacket or maybe a windbreaker."

"Hat?"

"No."

"Was he carrying anything?"

"I don't think so, but I think he was smoking."

"What makes you say that?"

"I don't know, he moved his hand toward his face."

"Did you see any smoke or a cigarette?"

"I'm sorry, but I only saw him for a second. I wasn't watching him; I had my eyes on Daisy."

I said, "Did you hear anything or smell something in the air?"

"Not really."

"Is there anything else? Even something you may think is insignificant."

"Not at the moment. But I'll think it over."

I handed her my card. "Please do. Call me with anything."

As Cox got back into her car, I said, "We never went to see the farmhouse that's here."

"It's nowhere near the crime scene."

"I know, but the access road runs parallel to the railroad tracks. And you always say that you never know unless you check it out."

"Fair enough, wiseass."

We took the narrow road for a quarter mile. The Murray farmhouse and a barn sat in the cul de sac. The red structures were old but freshly painted. An older man in overalls was turning the earth between the buildings.

"Excuse me, sir."

"Hi there."

"Do you work here?"

"Uh-huh, but can't call it work since they don't pay me. Guess it's more like volunteering, but I'm not complaining. I love this place."

I took my badge out. "We'd like to ask you a couple of questions."

"Sure." He extended his hand. "Frank Peters. I'm the Murray farmhouse ambassador."

We introduced ourselves. I said, "Were you here Tuesday, when the body of Mary Mercury was found?"

"No. I don't come in on Tuesdays. I volunteer at the lighthouse in the Highlands."

"Was anyone else working that day?"

"No." As he continued, I stared at the farmhouse, wondering how tall people were in the 1700s. The distance between the upper and lower windows looked no more than six feet.

"Can't attract volunteers. Nobody seems to care about the history of this place. It goes way back to 1770. Joseph Murray was a hero of sorts in the Revolutionary War and was shot dead right here. It's a shame—"

"What's that?" I pointed to the roof's eave.

"My son made me a camera. The damn hooligans who hang out in the park were putting so much graffiti on the house, I had to paint it once a month."

"You have recordings from that Tuesday?"

"Yeah, I turn it on when I leave."

"We're going to have to ask you to turn the tapes over to us."

"Okay, happy to do so."

We headed back to the office with a cassette.

WE WERE HANGING up our jackets when Sergeant Gesso came in the office. "How we doing, boys?"

Stone said, "Good, boss."

"The hotline give you anything to work with?"

"We're running them down but doesn't look like there's a breakthrough."

"We got to speed this up. I don't have to tell you the pressure I'm getting from Freehold."

"Come on, Sarge. Tell the suits to give us some space."

"I'd like to tell them to go to hell. But the kid's uncle is a free-holder, and they have oversight of the department. Not to mention providing the funds to operate this place."

"If he thinks it's so easy, ask him if he wants to do a ride-along."

"Don't be a wiseass, Stone. You want to exchange your paid time off to retire early?"

"Yeah, so?"

"Then close this case."

"Come on, Sarge. You wouldn't do that to me, would you?"

"I don't want to, but if it's not solved, I'm going to need you here. Now, get to work."

Gesso left. Stone kicked the trash, muttering a stream of curses. I took the tape and said, "I'm going to take a look at this."

Chapter Fifteen

The TV and tape player were on a gray metal cart. It reminded me of being in middle school. I popped the cassette in and hit play. The images were grainy at best and unreadable at times. It looked to be a long day. I hit pause and went to get a coffee.

On the way back, my favorite rookie intercepted me. Man, she a babe. She smiled and said, "I've been looking for you."

Uh-oh. Another warning about being careful for what you ask for. "How are you?"

"Doing great." She handed me a slip of paper. "Mr. Diller, the principal at Middletown South said to give you this."

"Thanks." It was the names of three girls and their contact information. Two of them we knew.

"Aren't high school girls a little too young for you?" She laughed and sashayed her way down the hall. God, she was near perfect.

I went back to the video room and watched fifteen minutes more. Bleary eyed, I hit pause and ejected the tape. It was time to get more background from Mary's friends.

Stone was still simmering when I walked in. "The principal called with the names of Mary's friends. We had Hart and

Wilson, but the teachers said she was close with Margaret Reilly. Figured it might be a good idea to talk to her."

"We need something. Let's go."

We pulled up to Reilly's cedar-shake ranch home. Walking to the door, the sound of an approaching train increased. The noise was a tradeoff for living within walking distance to the Middletown train station. As difficult it was for me to sleep, it was an exchange I could never make.

We sat on a leather couch in the family room. Sans the braces, Margaret Reilly was a younger version of her mother. They both had pixie noses and wore their hair short.

Stone said, "Your school said you and the victim were close."

"At school we were. We didn't hang out much outside of school. She was busy cheering, and I'm not into the whole school spirit thing."

"We're told she stopped cheering because she'd outgrown it."

"I don't know about that; she loved doing the gymnastics stuff. She was good at it. She tried to teach me to do cartwheels but forget it."

"Why do you think she left the squad?"

"She was tired of the backstabbing. A couple of the girls there were, well, some people say they're competitive, but they're just mean."

"Anyone in particular?"

"Natasha Borski. She's got some attitude. And she was super jealous of Mary."

"Anything she has done that we should know about?"

"Yeah, you probably know already, but she pushed Mary down the stairs."

"Where and when was this?"

"About a week or so ago, at school."

"Did she report it?"

"She did, but Natasha said she fell into her and it was an accident."

"Did she get hurt?"

"She banged up her knee pretty bad. You should look into her."

"We will. Is there anyone else who you think could possibly be responsible for what happened to her?"

She shrugged.

"Anything happen? Anyone she had a problem with?"

Another shrug.

"Come on, you can tell me. We'll check it out. No one will know who told us. You owe it to your friend."

"I don't want to say something but maybe Kenny Spencer."

"He's from your school?"

"No. He goes to North, and he's a real troublemaker."

"What makes you think he could be involved?"

"He really wanted Mary to go out with him. He asked her, like, ten times, but she said no."

"Was he upset about it?"

"Oh yeah. He said she better watch out."

"He threatened her?"

"Yep. I heard him say it."

"Did he do anything else that concerned you?"

"I didn't see him too much. He lives on the other side of town."

"How did he know Mary?"

"From football. He used to play for North but got kicked off the team."

"What about her boyfriend, Dominick Barrow?"

"It didn't last long. To me, it was like a brother-sister thing."

"How would you describe him?"

"I don't know, Dom's a little odd but he's okay."

"He didn't take the breakup good, did he?"

"He really had a crush on Mary, so he got down about it."

"Down enough to do something to her?"

"You think so?"

"I don't know him, that's why I'm asking you."

"After O.J. Simpson killed his wife, I guess anybody can do anything."

I REACHED INTO MY INBOX, picking up a sketch. The Keansburg police were looking for a man who tried to abduct kids on two occasions. The police artist had combined the descriptions from both eyewitnesses, who were both female and thirteen.

Showing the picture to Stone, I said, "You see this?"

"Yeah, I'd like somebody to give me ten minutes with that pervert."

"It could be the same guy who killed Mary."

"Nah, these girls are too young, it doesn't add up. And both attempts were by the amusement park. His MO doesn't match."

"Maybe, but he could've changed it up."

"Not these sociopaths."

"He knows they're watching the park. It's natural he'd change places."

"Let the Keansburg guys chase it down. If they come up with something, we'll get involved to see if there's a connection."

"You don't want to talk to these girls?"

My desk phone started ringing as he said, "We need to stay on the threads we got."

"Homicide, this is Detective Luca."

"Hi. This is Angie from Paws and Purrs Pet Shop."

"Thanks for returning my call, ma'am."

"You said this had something to do with the Mercury murder. My heart breaks for that family."

"It may be related, but we're not sure. You head up the Jersey chapter of the International Feline Association, don't you?"

"Yes. It's been ten years now. It's a lot of work and takes me away from the shop but I love it."

"I was curious to understand how high a cat can jump and

what, if any, kind of running start they'd need to, say, get to the height of a door handle."

"That would depend on the age and length of the cat. A younger, healthy cat can jump up to six times their length, about a maximum of eight feet or so."

"Eight feet?"

"Yes. They have very powerful muscles in their rear legs."

"How much of a running start would they need?"

"None. They crouch onto to their hind legs and explode up."

"So, reaching a door handle, where a cat could end up hanging itself, is a possibility?"

"Sure. That's why we recommend that if you're going to restrict a cat to a room, that you cat-proof it."

"What's that?"

"Putting a nubby sheet or sticky mat near the door. They don't like either of those surfaces."

I thanked her, hung up, and said, "It sounds like the Barrow kid was telling the truth about the cat. That was a lady from a cat association, said cats can hang themselves, and they recommend taking preventative measures."

"Then why'd the kid just come out and say it, then?"

"He was scared. Probably figured he'd get blamed for locking it in a room."

"And blowing up frogs? Instead of the cat lady, let's talk with the Natasha kid and the troublemaker."

Chapter Sixteen

Natasha Borski looked like a tomboy to me. She had wide shoulders and a square jaw. Her grandmother stood by, stirring a pot as we talked.

Stone said, "Tell me about your relationship with Mary Mercury."

"There's nothing to say. We were on the cheering squad together."

"Someone said you were jealous of her. Were you?"

The grandmother may have had a thick Russian accent, but with the question she stopped moving the ladle around.

"Why would I be jealous of her? I'm much better at cheering than she was. She didn't like it. She was very competitive."

"You didn't like Mary, did you?"

She shrugged.

"Is that why you pushed her down the stairs?"

"Don't tell me you're going to start with the whole stairs thing, are you?"

"Just tell me what happened."

"Nothing happened, we were going down the stairs, and she was in front me. I tripped and fell into her."

"Did you fall as well?"

"No, I caught the railing and saved myself."

"No one was in the stairwell?"

"No, just us."

"If you didn't like her, what were you doing alone with her?"

Surprise flashed across her face. "I don't know, it just ended up like that."

"Mary told people that you tried to hurt her by pushing her down the stairs."

"Not true. It's her word against mine."

"Where were you after school, the afternoon of Tuesday, October tenth?"

"What? You think I did this? That's crazy, man."

"Answer the question."

"I was here, with Baba."

The grandmother said, "Is true."

While the alibi may have been tainted, Natasha had probably pushed Mary down the stairs. That said, neither of us thought she had killed her rival.

———

IT WAS on to Kenny Spencer. He lived just off Route 36 in a manufactured home. It looked like a double-wide and sat on a pie-shaped lot. As soon as his mother opened the door, we were hit with the smell of cigarette smoke. And she didn't even have a cigarette in her hand.

She pulled out a pack as soon as we introduced ourselves and was puffing as we headed to the kitchen. The house was neat and nicer than expected. She opened a rear door. Her son was working on a motorcycle that looked months from rideable.

Wiry, with a sharp nose and slicked-back hair, Kenny Spencer smelled defiant. I noticed a newish cut on his right hand as he crossed his arms over his chest. Sucking on a Marlboro, his mother stood behind him.

Stone said, "We want to ask you some questions about Mary Mercury."

"What about her?"

"We understand you asked her out several times."

"Yeah, so?"

"And she said no."

"I didn't wanna be with her anyway."

"Then why'd you ask her?"

"Screw with her head. She thought she was something special. All those kids who go to South, they think they're better than us."

"We have witnesses who said you threatened her."

"I was just trying to scare her. It was nothing."

"You hang out in Fairview Cemetery, don't you?"

"Sometimes."

"It's close to Poricy Park, where Mary was found. Were you there Tuesday?"

She put a hand on her son's shoulder. "Hold on a minute there. Are you accusing my son of some kind of involvement in the poor girl's death?"

"We're just trying to obtain information. Nobody is accusing anybody of anything."

"Well, it sure sounds like it."

"Why don't you tell us what you were doing on Tuesday, October tenth?"

"I don't know. I was here most of the day, working on my bike."

"You weren't in school?"

"My son was suspended for fighting."

"Is that the first time?"

"That's none of your business."

I said, "Where'd you get that cut?"

"Oh, this? It's nothing, got it working on the bike."

"Exactly how?"

"Uh, I was trying to get a bolt off, and my hand slipped and hit the frame."

"Mrs. Spencer, were you home on Tuesday the tenth?"

"For the most part."

"How about the afternoon between two and four?"

"Yes, I was here."

"Was your son?"

She hesitated. "Yes, Kenny was here, working on that damn bike his father gave him."

We didn't have much more than rumors and a kid that was one mistake away from delinquency. We finished up, and Stone was out the door. I turned to the kid and said, "Being a tough guy is not going to get you anywhere. Stay in school and keep your nose clean, or we're going to get to know each other really well."

As soon as we got back to the office, Stone spied a pink message sitting on his desk. He picked it up. "Boss wants an update on the case."

"You want me to come along?"

"Nah, check and see if there's anything in the juvie file on Spencer."

"But it'd be sealed."

"I know that. Look for any arrests. Something to suggest we should dig into him."

He walked out, and I called the records division and made the request. I had nothing to do. I grabbed the cassette and went to the video room.

The activity by the Murray farmhouse amounted to one rabbit and a pesky crow who kept flying into view. As the time stamp hit 2:31 p.m., a kid came into view. It looked like Dominick Barrow. I paused the tape.

Had we asked him if he had been at the park? Not directly. He'd claimed to be home playing a video game. Was it really him?

I got closer to the screen. If it wasn't, it was someone who looked incredibly similar. What was he doing there? Hitting play, I watched him move out of view, heading in the direction of the railroad tracks. I rewound the tape and hit play. He didn't have the pocketbook. Unless it was under his jacket.

He walked offscreen again, and I let it run, hoping he'd come into view, or maybe Mary would be caught on tape. At 3:07, a male figure passed quickly in and out of view. Who was it?

I rewound it and paused on the image. He was wearing a dark jacket and jeans. Was this the person the jogger and poodle lady had seen? I let the tape run until four thirty. There was no further activity.

We had something. I picked up the phone.

Chapter Seventeen

"Stone, it's Frank."

"Where the hell are you?"

"In the video room. We got something on the farmhouse video."

"What are you talking about?"

"Looks like Barrow and another guy were at the park during the time Mary was murdered."

"I'll be right there."

I rewound the video to right before Barrow appeared, and seconds later, Stone, breathing heavily, barged into the room.

"Let me see that movie."

I hit play and he said, "This is crap. I can hardly see anything."

"Watch, I think that's Barrow. See?"

"It's frigging him. He lied to us."

"Keep watching." Barrow exited the screen and I hit fast-forward. "The other guy is going to appear any second now." I pointed. "There he is."

As quickly as the male came into view, he disappeared.

"Get that part back on."

We watched it and froze it, but we couldn't see anything but the person's back.

"I wanna see Barrow again. Run it slow. He might have the pocketbook."

"I checked that out. He wasn't carrying anything visible."

"Let me determine that."

We viewed it four more times but didn't learn anything new. Stone said, "Let's go see that lying prick."

———

STONE WAS quiet as I drove. It felt like he was thinking through a line of questioning. His style was more shoot from the hip than contemplative, but maybe it was all an act. I needed to know what it was because he knew how to close cases.

I pulled onto Ravine Road and stopped in front of the Barrow residence. Stone said, "Take the recorder. I want this documented."

A TV was on somewhere. The sound of an explosion sounded as Mrs. Barrow showed us into the living room. She said, "Let me get Dominick."

I felt for the woman and could smell her fear that her son had done something horrible. The TV went quiet. Mrs. Barrow led her son into the room. As they sat, Stone said, "Hello, Dom."

"Hi."

"We have a couple more questions."

"Okay."

I pulled out the recorder and put it on the table, saying, "This interview is going to be recorded."

Mrs. Barrow said, "Recorded? Why would you record it?"

Stone said, "To keep things straight. It's all about protecting you, not us. We can't make anything up. Really, it's for your protection."

It was line I would adopt, making it a part of my repertoire.

"Going back to the afternoon of Tuesday, October tenth. Can you remember that day?"

"Of course, it was the day Mary died."

"Yes. That afternoon, after school, what did you do?"

"I told you, I was home, did some homework, and played video games."

"You're sure?"

"Yes. Why?"

"Did you go to Poricy Park that afternoon?"

"No."

"Are you sure?"

"Mom, why don't they believe me?"

"It's okay, Dominick. Just try and answer their questions."

"You want to know why we don't believe you?"

"I guess so."

"Because we have you on tape at the park."

"What?"

His mother gasped. "Dominick, were you there?"

"No, I wasn't. I swear. They're making this up."

"The Murray farmhouse has video surveillance of you at 2:31 p.m. What were you doing there?"

"I wasn't there."

"I think you're lying."

"Hold on now. My son is telling you he wasn't there and that's it."

"How do explain the video?"

"I have no idea. There's probably a problem with the camera or something."

There was a slight chance she was right, but it was pinhead sized. I said, "What were you wearing that day?"

"Uh, I don't know. Jeans for sure, but I can't remember the shirt I was wearing."

Stone said, "I don't care about your shirt. What jacket did you have on?"

"My Members Only jacket."

"What color?"

"Dark blue, it's almost black."

"You were in the park the day Mercury was murdered."

"Leave him alone! He said he wasn't."

"Come clean, kid. It'll be a lot easier on you and your mother."

Mrs. Barrow stood. "I . . . I want you to leave. Okay?"

"Are you sure about that?"

"Shut that thing off!"

"I'd suggest speaking with your son. Tell him it's always better to tell the truth."

"Get out, now."

"Fine, if that's what you want, but we'll be back."

We walked to the car in silence as most cops are taught. You never knew who was listening. I started the car up and said, "What do you think?"

"Why? You don't think the kid did it?"

"I'm not sure. I don't like the fact he was at the park and wouldn't fess up about it."

"That's because he doesn't want to put himself at the scene."

"Maybe, but what about the other male at the park?"

"Barrow could have had an accomplice. They go in separately, hide out. Maybe Barrow asked Mercury to meet him there."

"Why would he want to involve someone else?"

"Because he's a kid and he's stupid."

"I can't see the accomplice angle on this."

"Either way, Barrow had a hand, or two, around her neck, and killed Mercury."

"Why would he do that?"

"Why? She dumped him. We know he was smitten with the victim. When she tells him it's over, he tries to get back with her, and she gets annoyed he won't leave her alone. That sets off Barrow. We know Barrow has a temper."-."

"There's no evidence of that."

"What about the cat? And blowing up frogs?"

"The cat thing was an accident. You know how many kids put frogs on the road hoping they get squished by cars? I'll go along with he was upset the relationship was over, so go from there."

"Barrow arranges to meet her in the park. When Mercury gets there, he suggests they take a walk. He tried to convince her to get back together but she rejects him. She tries to get away, and he grabs her from behind and chokes her to death."

"Where'd he get the rope?"

"He could have had it with him."

"It was premeditated?"

"Probably not. I think he just got worked up and snapped. But he could've gotten the idea in one of those violent video games he plays and took a rope with him."

"Why would he take the pocketbook, then?"

"To make it look like something else happened."

"What you're saying sounds awfully speculative to me."

"You think so, huh? Don't worry, we'll get more evidence when we do a search. You'll see."

"You want a warrant to search the Barrow home?"

"Why not?"

"I don't think we'll get one at this point."

"We have nothing else going. They'll give me one."

Chapter Eighteen

Stone had gone to see Gesso, asking me to get started on the warrant application. I completed what I could. We needed probable cause for a judge to sign off on it, and I felt we weren't there yet.

Mary had ended the relationship with Barrow; it was one he wanted to continue. I'm sure the kid was hurt. But strangling wasn't like firing a gun; it wasn't over in a second. There'd be a struggle, and the killer would have to have ice running through his veins to complete the act. I was good at reading people, and this kid didn't feel like a killer.

There was no denying Barrow was at the park. And he lied about it. Why? The thought Mrs. Barrow had, that the camera might have been malfunctioning came into my head. I made a note to get it checked out as Stone walked in.

"Gesso is on board. He said put whatever we have in the warrant; he'll call Freehold. Worse comes to worst, they'll see we're doing something."

"I guess you're right."

"Guess?"

Stone recited what he wanted to look for in the Barrow home. It included rope or similar articles, Barrow's clothing, his dairy, any correspondence with Mary, articles thought to belong to Mary, and the kitchen sink.

For probable cause, we had Barrow at the crime scene, but Stone exaggerated, insinuating that Barrow was a violent person, was obsessed with Mary, and had threatened her.

"You sure you want to put it that way?"

"What's the matter? We're just adding a little juice."

"It's not fair to the kid."

"Look, we need to do the search. Let's see what we find."

"I don't know. It doesn't feel right."

"It's a logical step; trust me on this."

"All right. I'm going to send someone down to the Murray farmhouse to get the camera."

"Why?"

"I want to make sure it's operating properly."

"That's a waste of time."

"If the video gets introduced into court, we'll need it anyway to prove it's working right."

"You're thinking like a lawyer. But go ahead, I'm sure it works fine."

It was weird, but I was hoping Stone was wrong. "It might be a good idea to get pictures of Barrow and the mystery man made off the tape and show them to the women at the park."

"I already asked the lab to make 'em up. Said we'd have them this afternoon."

"Perfect."

"Take the application to the suits. I'm gonna let Gesso know we're sending it up."

WE HAD two pictures of Barrow and the other male in the park. It concerned me that the side of Barrow's face was visible but only the rear of the mystery man. Eyewitnesses were double edged; they were critical in identifying a suspect but were often unreliable.

We pulled up in front of the poodle lady's house. I said, "I don't know what to expect."

"We just need one of them to finger Barrow."

"I'd feel better if they both did."

"We got the video. If one of these women confirm it, we're on our way."

Clara Cox came to the door. Daisy stuck her snoot around her owner's leg "Come on in."

I said, "Thank you, ma'am. This will only take a minute."

Stone said, "You told us you saw a male in the park around the time the girl was murdered. I have a couple of photos for you to look at. See if any of them look like him."

He handed both Barrow images to her. "Is this him?"

Cox shifted her head between the pictures. "I don't think."

"Take another look."

"I can't tell."

"But it could be him."

"I guess so."

He exchanged the photos for the ones of the unidentified male. "I know these are not helpful, but take a look anyway."

Stone led so well he could take the poodle into a dog show.

"Hmmm. He looks familiar."

"But you can't see his face."

"I know, but something about him rings a bell."

Stone swapped photos again. "Take another look at these. Does he look familiar?"

"I don't know. This is really hard."

"You think it would be easier if we had him in a lineup?"

"In person? He wouldn't see me, would he?"

"No, don't worry. It'd be anonymous."

"Okay."

"We'll let you know. Thanks for your time."

We hopped in the car. I said, "That wasn't helpful."

"We'll see what happens when we do a lineup."

Stone had to know that the odds would increase that Cox would pick out Barrow because subconsciously she'd recall the photos.

"A defense attorney would ask to suppress it, and a judge would agree."

"I don't work for those slimebags. Besides, we're just collecting info at this point."

WENDY O'ROURKE HAD a pink sweater and jeans on. Her face had the healthy glow of a fitness buff. I said, "Thank you for seeing us on short notice."

"It's okay. I wasn't busy."

Stone said, "We have photos of two people in the park who we believe may be involved in the murder. Take a look, and see which one you recognize."

He handed the Barrow photos to the jogger.

She brought the pictures closer and shook her head. "I don't think it was him."

"Don't think or don't know?"

"I'd hate to say either way because I just don't remember."

"Try these."

She looked at the mystery man's back. "He's the same size, but it's just the back of him. Do you have any of his face?"

"No, that's all we got." He exchanged pictures. "Take another look at this guy."

"This is really hard, and I'd feel bad making a mistake."

"Don't worry about that. It's not like we're relying only on your say-so."

"He could be the guy, but let me see the other one again."

Stone handed them to her and she said, "You know, they both look a little like the guy I saw."

Chapter Nineteen

I slid into a booth at Steak and Ale. Debra didn't say anything. Instead, she forked another piece of fried calamari.

"I got tied up. Things are moving fast."

"You should've called."

"I tried, but you left the house already. How's the calamari?"

"Just okay."

"Did you order yet?"

"Yep. I got a cheddar cheeseburger and onion rings coming."

I flagged down a waiter and ordered the same but with fries and a beer.

"So what happened today?"

I told her about the warrant and showing the witnesses the pictures we had made.

"If you find anything at the Barrow kid's house, that'll be it."

"I guess so, but I don't know."

"What's bothering you?"

"I'm not convinced the kid did it, but Stone, he seems, I don't know, too focused on him."

"He's got a lot of experience."

"I know." I picked up a ring of calamari and said, "Let's change the subject. I need a break from the case."

———

THE WARRANT CAME through at ten the next morning. By noon, I was standing in front of the Barrow home with Stone, a pair of property crime investigators, and a uniformed officer. A gust of wind stripped leaves off the oak trees as I rang the bell. It took two rings to get a response.

Mrs. Barrow was wearing exercise clothes including a pair of maroon leggings. Her face had a sheen to it. Mouth open, she stared at the contingent of law enforcement. I handed her the warrant.

"I'm sorry, ma'am, but we have a court order to conduct a search of your home."

"A search? Are you kidding me?"

"No, ma'am. I have to ask you to step aside."

"I can't go into my own house?"

"No, ma'am."

"But it's freezing out here. I'm all sweaty."

"You can sit in the squad car." The uniform escorted her to one, and we entered the home. Stone said, "I'm going to the kid's room. You check the main living quarters and you two, one search the garage and the other, the shed out back."

I headed into the family room. Jane Fonda was on the TV doing a stretch. Unsure what to look for but certain I'd know it when I saw it, I rummaged through the entertainment center. A stack of video games sat next to a Nintendo console. I went through a couple of them: *Donkey Kong, Mortal Combat, Yoshi's Island*. They weren't all violent.

On my way into the kitchen, I nearly collided with Stone coming out of the kid's bedroom. Empty handed, he said, "You find anything?"

"No. You?"

He shook his head and went down the basement stairs.

I didn't expect to find anything and didn't. Except a nice mix of pasta boxes, the kitchen had nothing of interest. I checked inside the bathroom vanity, but other than a bottle of Scope and four rolls of toilet paper, it was empty. As I headed to the living room, footsteps sounded from the basement stairs.

The door swung open. Stone said, "Bingo." With a screwdriver, he was holding a coil of rope. It looked to be jute.

"Where was it?"

"Lying on a workbench."

"You think that's what was used?"

"Yep."

"But it's too long."

"See here." He pointed to the end of the rope. "A piece was cut off."

I didn't know what that meant and said, "The lab can tell us if the fibers match."

"It's going to match. Trust me. Get one of those big paper bags out of the trunk."

On the way to the car, I saw Mrs. Barrow in the back seat of the patrol car. She was crying. I couldn't imagine how she was feeling and didn't see it getting any better for her.

THREE PHONE CALLS CAME IN. Stone picked them up on the first ring, hoping it was the laboratory. The sarge had instructed them to prioritize the rope. Another call came in.

"Stone. Homicide."

"Hello, Robert. It's Eugene."

"How's it going, Gene?"

"Just wanted to let you know the Barrows have retained Vic

D'Amato. We'll need to keep him informed of any developments, if we can."

"We're about to arrest his new client, but I'll let you know. Thanks for the heads-up."

He hung up. "Barrow got himself a lawyer. They didn't make the best choice with D'Amato."

"Did you say we're about to arrest Barrow?"

He reached for the phone. "Stone. Homicide." He listened, and his face broke into a smile. "I look forward to it. Thanks."

He hung up. "The rope is jute, and the diameter is in the range of the type used to strangle the Mercury kid."

"Can they identify if the fibers on Mary's neck match the rope you found?"

"He's faxing over the report." He headed for the door. "I gotta tell Gesso and get an arrest warrant going."

The fax machine started spitting out a page. It was the lab report. I read the findings. It raised more questions than it answered.

Chapter Twenty

It was only my second homicide case, but I believed we didn't have enough for an arrest. Wondering what Stone had told Gesso, he sauntered into the office.

"The sarge is on board."

"With what?"

"Arresting Barrow."

"That's crazy. The lab didn't give us anything." I slid the report on his desk. Stone looked it over.

"It's the same material and diameter."

"Did you read the part that says it's a common type of house-hold rope."

"Yeah. Let me ask you, do you have a rope like this?"

"No. But that's beside the point."

"What do you think the odds are that Barrow, who was upset over a relationship with the victim and was at the park, would have a rope matching the one used?"

"The relationship thing is puppy-love crap. They're kids, for Christ's sake."

"And the violent behavior?"

"You talking about the cat? If you are, it could have been an accident."

"Not in my book. And don't forget about blowing up frogs. Don't you know that the FBI says there's a link between abusing animals and murder?"

"We don't have enough to arrest the kid. Let's slow this down, look more into Barrow and chase down the other guy there that day."

"In my book we have enough. Plus, we don't have time. The brass is up my ass, and I want to make my exit with a clean slate."

"So the solution is to put a kid, who may be innocent, behind bars?"

"What, did you forget that he was at the scene? And lied about it?"

"No."

"You had the camera checked out. It's working fine. So what was he doing there?"

"I don't know, but there could be an explanation. Maybe he was smoking pot or doing something he doesn't want to admit."

"A couple of nights behind bars will give him the chance to come clean."

"You can't arrest him."

"Really?" Stone stood. "Who are you to be telling me that? I was closing cases while you were playing Little League, kid."

I kept my mouth shut as he stormed out. I needed to do something, but what? The real answer was to locate the mystery man or find more evidence supporting it was Barrow. It wasn't unrealistic to ask Stone for two weeks to do a deeper dive into the kid.

Getting more time from Stone was unlikely at this point. Pushing hard against him ruined that chance. I could go to Captain Kilihan or Gesso, but going around a direct report would stain my reputation before I had a chance to build one.

What about going to the press? It wasn't clear how they'd

react to what I had to say. There was also no way to do it anonymously. The details I had were held by Stone and I. As soon as I leaked it, my career in law enforcement would be over.

It was a lose-lose situation. Was it worth risking my career over? I didn't believe Barrow did it but outside of working the case didn't know what to do about it.

The only thing to do was get back to the fundamentals. I'd start with Mary's parents. Picking up the phone to call them, Stone and Kilihan walked in the office. Stone closed the door, and Kilihan sat on the corner of my desk.

"How you doing, kid?"

"All right, Captain."

"I understand you're going rebel on us."

"Rebel? No, sir."

"Stoney was telling me you're pushing back on making an arrest."

"I'm just—"

"You see, this place is one big team. This place don't work if we don't have a chain of command. You get that?"

"Yes, sir."

"We can't have a bunch of renegades saying they want to do something their way. Does that make sense?"

"Yes, sir. It's just that—"

"When a senior officer, especially one with Stoney's record, says go left, you go left. You understand that?"

"Yes. I was only trying to obtain more evidence against Barrow before we made an arrest. I want to be sure we make the right call."

Stone came over. "I want to be sure as well. That's why I want to bring him in."

"But we can talk to him here, without arresting him."

"He'll lawyer up. D'Amato isn't a fan of letting his clients talk."

Kilihan said, "Stoney's right. The kid will get shook up when he's in a cell. We make it real for him. Maybe offer a deal if he comes clean. I've seen it a million times; scaring someone is the quickest way to get to the truth."

"I understand, sir."

"That's good. See, Stoney, I told you Luca was a team player."

A wave of nausea washed over me. But it paled as a tsunami of regret hit me.

Chapter Twenty-One

As soon as the captain left, Stone said, "Let's get a team together for the arrest."

"I'm not sure we need a team. The kid is sixteen."

"You can never be sure how the parents are going to react."

"I can't see that. Besides, we need to call their lawyer, don't we?"

"Yeah, go ahead and do that, and I'll get a couple of cars together. Tell him we'll be there in two hours to take the kid."

"He'll probably want to bring him in and surrender."

"You know what, hold off on that call. You can make it right before we head over."

"Are you sure?"

On his way out the door, he said, "Never been surer."

He seemed rock solid, and I was doubting everything, including my decision to be a homicide detective. I considered going to Gesso, but he was an organization man, and if his captain and lead detective were behind something, he wouldn't undermine them.

I rolled around going to the press, but at this point, it would be too late to marshal public opinion. Barrow was going to be arrested and that was that. I hoped his lawyer was better than Stone seemed to indicate.

Stone breezed in. "Make your call and then we're rolling."

I dialed the phone and was passed to Barrow's lawyer.

"Mr. D'Amato, Detective Luca, with the Middletown Police. I'm calling about Dominick Barrow."

"Hello, Detective. What about my client?"

"I'm notifying you that he is going to be arrested for suspicion of murdering Mary Mercury."

"That's outlandish. Mr. Barrow is a minor. Let me arrange a surrender. How about tomorrow morning?"

"I'm afraid that won't work; things are in motion."

"Give me time to get to their home."

"You'd better hurry."

"I'm on my way. And since he's a minor, I'd appreciate you not calling the press. There's no need to turn this into a circus."

"I understand. Goodbye."

I hung up. "He said he's heading down there and reminded us not to call the press."

"Too late for that."

"What do you mean?"

"This is a big case; they got a right to know what we're doing about it."

"You're gonna ruin the kid's reputation."

"He did it to himself. Let's go."

FOLLOWING TWO PATROL CARS, I turned onto Ravine Drive. A white van with the ABC logo on it was parked across the street from the Barrow home. It made me wonder when Stone had tipped them off.

I'd made plenty of arrests but never a minor. Reaching for the bell, my hand shook. Mrs. Barrow was in a housecoat looking twenty years older than the first day we met. She looked as if we'd stepped off a flying saucer.

Stone said, "Get your son, ma'am."

"Why can't you leave him alone?"

"If you don't get him, we have the authority to enter. He's under arrest."

She staggered, and I reached for her arm. "You can't take my baby!"

Stone brushed past her. "Dominick Barrow! Come to the door."

"Leave him alone!"

"Mom?" Dominick came running down the hallway. "What's going on?"

Stone said, "Dominick Barrow, you're under arrest for the murder of Mary Mercury."

"But I didn't do anything."

"Dominick!"

He tried to run to his mother, but Stone corralled him. He turned him around, slapping cuffs on him as he read him his rights. Mrs. Barrow fell onto her knees, emitting a wail that chilled me. Dominick began to sob uncontrollably. I couldn't look at the kid.

Stone said, "Put him the car." A uniform stepped up and grabbed the kid's elbow. As they left the house, I noticed a cameraman recording the entire episode. To his left stood a reporter with a microphone.

Stone marched out, and I followed him, staring at my shoes. Before we hit the street, someone said, "Detective Stone, can we have a word?" It was the newsman. Stone told me to wait in the car.

I watched Stone talk to the reporter, expecting his face to break into a smile. There was a chance the correspondent knew him from a previous case, but that was beside the point: he'd set the scene up.

I'd only worked one other case with him. He could have been a publicity hound or was looking to leave in the spotlight, cementing his legacy. The patrol car carrying the kid left the block. An officer held back Mrs. Barrow as the patrol car drove off. Stone didn't even glance at it.

He nodded to the reporter, starting toward the car. As soon as he closed the door, I said, "That was ugly."

"Comes with the territory. You should know that."

What I knew was families were torn apart when a member committed a serious crime. This felt more like a mother being stripped of custody. I needed a shower.

BARROW WAS BEING BOOKED when we got back. I quickly called Debra to let her know it was going to be a long night. Hanging up, the DA came in.

"D'Amato is making a stink over the way you brought the Barrow kid in. Said he asked to have him surrender."

Stone said, "Whatever. I didn't want to take the chance the kid would run. His father has a travel agency."

"Be prepared he's going to let off some steam."

"Instead of worrying about me, he should concentrate on his client."

"Just let him say his piece."

"Okay."

"And don't talk to the kid without him in the room. I don't care if both his parents are there. It won't look good."

Stone looked like a five-year-old who'd been told Santa Claus had died.

Chapter Twenty-Two

An orange jumpsuit hung off Dominick Barrow as he shuffled toward an interview room. His legs were shackled and his hands cuffed behind his back. He looked as vulnerable as a newborn.

D'Amato greeted Barrow, putting an arm around his shoulder as he led him into the room. The lawyer had politely scolding us for the way the arrest occurred and for the unnecessary media coverage of it. After the tactful spanking, he asked for time to consult with his client before we questioned him.

Stone seemed calm, but he reminded me of a swan: calm above the lake but continual motion below the surface. There was no surprise in him stating his desire to ask the questions and I nodded in agreement.

Ten minutes of small talk crawled by before the door swung open. D'Amato said, "We're ready when you are."

Following Stone in, I took a seat across from D'Amato. Feeling more like a UN observer in a war zone than a detective, I said hello to both of them and turned the recorder on. After stating the formalities, Stone said, "You hungry or anything?"

Barrow shook his head.

When Stone followed with, "Can I get anyone anything?" I

wondered whether he was going to play *good cop-bad cop* by himself.

After more nodding Stone said, "May I call you Dominick?"

"Sure."

"Good. Now, Dominick, you know why you're here?"

"No. I didn't do anything wrong."

As he swept away a tear with the back of his hand, Stone said, "We believe you strangled Mary Mercury."

"No I didn't! I would never hurt Mary."

"You were upset over the end of your relationship, weren't you?"

"Yeah."

"And you wanted to get back at her for hurting you, didn't you?"

"No, that's not true. I didn't do anything!"

"It could have been unintentional; we understand that. A lot of times, things spin out of control and stuff happens. Just tell us, and we'll get this sorted out for you."

"My client has repeatedly denied the allegations. Next question, please."

"Were you at Poricy Park on Tuesday, October tenth between the hours of one and four p.m.?"

"No, I told you that before."

"How do explain your presence on a surveillance tape, then?"

"My client maintains he was not there. If this goes any further, we'll explore the validity of the recording, at the appropriate time."

"Trust me, Counselor, it's as real as it gets."

"Do you have another question, or are we finished here?"

"Dominick, do you have a pet?"

"No."

"Most kids want a dog or cat. Would you like to have a pet?"

He shrugged.

"You don't like pets, do you?"

"I don't know."

"Is that why you kill them?"

"Detective, let me remind you, if you're going to make wild accusations, you'll have to back them up with hard evidence. May we move on, please?"

"Where did you buy the rope, Dominick?"

"I didn't buy any rope."

"Where did you get the rope that you strangled Mary Mercury with?"

"I told you! I didn't do it!"

"Oh, I know you did it."

Dominick began to sob, and D'Amato asked for a ten-minute break. We stepped outside. I said, "The kid is sticking to his story."

"Give it time. After a night in the can, they'll beg us to get him into the juvie system."

"I'm sure D'Amato is going to push for an arraignment tonight."

Stone smiled. "The court is really backed up."

"Let me grab a couple of bottles of water."

"I'm gonna take a leak."

When we got back, D'Amato signaled their readiness. I handed out the water, restarting the recorder. Stone said,

"Back to the rope used in the murder. Now, Dominick, how do you explain our finding a coil that matches the one used to kill Miss Mercury, in your basement?"

"I don't know. Maybe my father bought it."

"Okay, your dad bought it. How long a piece did you cut from the coil?"

"I didn't cut anything."

"Come on, Dom, it's not a crime to cut a length of rope."

"I . . . I didn't even know it was there." He hung his head and sobbed. "Why doesn't anybody believe me?"

"My client is upset. I'd like some time alone with him. But we're done for the day."

"If that's the way you want to play it, we'll resume the interview tomorrow."

"I want to see my parents."

"Sorry, kid. Not until you've been arraigned."

"I'd consider it a personal favor, Detective, if you'd find a way to give him five minutes with his parents."

"I'd love to help you, Counselor, but rules are rules, and I don't make them."

The kid's wail matched his mother's. I hurried out of the room. I didn't want to talk to anybody. What I needed to do was process what I witnessed. Was this kid telling the truth or not? I headed to the cafeteria for a coffee wondering why the kid lied about being in the park.

Passing the front desk, I heard, "There's one of them." It was Mrs. Barrow. She said, "Where's our son? We want to see our boy."

As I sped up, the father shouted, "You bastards are going to pay for this!"

Chapter Twenty-Three

An episode of *Friends* was on, and Debra was in my recliner when I walked in the door. "Hey, sorry I'm late."

"What's the matter? You look like you lost your puppy or something."

"Rough day. We arrested the Barrow kid, and it wasn't pretty."

"You talked to him?"

"Yep."

"You think he did it?"

"I don't know, but we didn't have enough to drag him in, especially in cuffs. His parents went ballistic."

"How old is he?"

"Sixteen, but today he looked like he was twelve."

"Geez, I can't imagine. What's next?"

"He's not going to be arraigned till tomorrow."

"How's his lawyer?"

"First time I met him. Seems nice, but I think he's waiting to see what we have on him."

"The kid will get out on bail, won't he?"

"I can't see a judge denying it. The only wild card is the father has a travel agency."

"They think they'll run?"

"I don't think so, but it's a possibility. If the kid has a passport, he'll have to surrender it."

"He'll be released."

"Yeah, but it's not over for him. Either way, the kid is in the system now, and it'll leave a mark on him."

"Well, if he did it, he's where he belongs."

THE PHONE on my nightstand rang. Blinking, I saw it was 4:35 a.m. and answered.

"Who is it?"

"Sergeant Gesso."

I bolted upright. "What's going on, Sarge?"

"You better get in. I just got a call on the Barrow kid."

"What about him?"

"Looks like suicide."

"Are you shitting me?"

"Wish I was."

"I'm on my way."

I got out of bed.

"What's going on, Frank?"

"Go back to sleep. I'm going in early; something is going on with the Barrow kid."

A wave of nausea hit me as I pulled on my pants. I put my shoulder holster on and ran to the car. If I was going to throw up, I didn't want Debra to see me doing it.

STONE'S CAR was in the parking lot. It was crowded for five in the morning. The jail was connected to the station by a long corridor. I signed in, and a steel door creaked open. Claustrophobia increasing with each step, I went down the stairs to the cell level.

Waiting for a gate to open, I saw Stone and two other officers standing in the foyer outside the cell area. It was quieter than a funeral parlor. Approaching, the smell of urine hit me.

"The kid . . . committed suicide?"

Stone said, "Yeah, he hanged himself."

"Oh, man, this is crazy."

"See for yourself."

I followed Stone past two cells. The prisoner's eyes were glued on us as we closed in on a cell whose door was open.

I saw a sliver of a hanging body, hesitating before I got a full view. Bile sprayed the back of my throat. I blinked.

Eyes bulging, Dominick Barrow was hanging from the light fixture.

I tore my eyes away and surveyed the room. On the floor lay a bedsheet that had been ripped into strips. His lace-less sneakers were tucked under the bunk. On the bed was a piece of paper.

Was it a suicide note? I walked in and bent over. It was blank.

"This kid shouldn't have been here. He should be home, safe in his bed. I don't understand it. How the hell did this happen?"

Stone said, "The kid used a bedsheet. Looks like he lassoed it over the fixture—"

"I know that. I mean why didn't anybody see what was going on?"

"McKlowski said it was a crazy night. The two guys in the next cell were beating the shit out of each other, and they had to take them to the hospital. In the other cell, an asshole was pissing all over the floor."

"And nobody checks on the kid?"

"They were shorthanded. It's a tough break."

"Tough break? The kid is here a couple of hours and he's dead."

"Don't forget why he was here."

"We still have to prove he did it."

"Yeah, well, right now we got to write this one up. I don't see any evidence of foul play, but take a look yourself."

"Who found him?"

"Guard named Brown. He came back from dealing with the fight, and when he did a round, he saw him."

"What time did they break up the fight?"

"We'll have to look at the time the medic unit left, but Brown said it was two fifteen."

"And he waited two hours to do a round? That's bullshit. I want to talk with the other prisoners."

"I did already. Looks like it was a pretty normal night. Besides the two brain surgeons beating the crap out of each other, there was a pervert making sexual comments, and the moron who took a crap on the floor and pissed through the bars. Oh yeah, some guy with mental issues was screaming his head off so bad, they put him the rubber room. Like I said, all around, it was a normal night."

"Normal? A corrections officer might consider it typical, but we put a sixteen-year-old, from the suburbs, in with them."

"We do it all the time."

"Please don't give me that excuse. I told you I was against it."

"It's not our fault this happened. Our job is to bring 'em in. It's up to corrections to keep them in one piece."

"Who the hell is going to explain this to the parents? I'm not doing it."

"Me neither. Let Gesso figure it out. Here comes Richter."

The medical examiner and two of his assistants sidled up. He looked over the scene for a minute and said, "Put a plastic sheet on the floor and take him down."

Wiping perspiration off my lip, I said, "I gotta take a bad leak."

My stomach was gurgling. I went straight to the sink and turned the water on. Swallowing hard, I cupped my hands under the stream. I wasn't fast enough. Grabbing the sides of the sink with both hands, I vomited.

Chapter Twenty-Four

"Shut it off. What's the matter with you?"

"I can't stop watching."

"Maybe that's why you can't sleep."

Debra grabbed the remote and shut off another interview with the Barrow parents.

"They filed a suit against the department and Middletown."

"How much they looking for?"

"Fifty million."

"Wow. That's crazy."

"I hope they get it. This never should have happened. I didn't have the balls to stop it."

"Stop beating yourself up."

"I can't, and because I didn't speak up, the kid is dead."

"That's not true. You said you told them they didn't have enough, didn't you?"

"Yeah, but I should have pushed back, gone to Gesso or the press."

"You think that would've worked?"

"I don't know, but it's beside the point. I knew it was wrong and didn't do as much as I could've to stop it."

"You're not being fair. The kid was arrested for murder."

"So? Does that mean it's okay that he's dead? And we don't even know for sure. Isn't he allowed to try and clear his name?"

"Then why'd he kill himself if he wasn't guilty?"

"Bottom line was he couldn't find a way out. Barrow was scared, felt like there was nothing anybody could do to help him. He was getting a lot of heat at school. He didn't want to go the last two days. Said the school was watching him."

"Oh, come on. They were watching him?"

"They had to. If they didn't and something happened, they'd be responsible."

"I guess so. I don't know why kids have to be so mean. You think our children would do that?"

I didn't want to tell her that at that moment, seeing the sorrow the Barrows were experiencing, reduced my already low desire to be a parent to zero.

"It's all about the peer pressure."

"Damn bullies are what they are."

Hearing the word bully brought Stone to mind. In a round-about way, he had bullied the system by putting Barrow behind bars. I was an unwilling accomplice but an accessory nonetheless. A court of law wasn't what I was concerned about. It was whispering from the guilt monkey perched on my shoulder that made me anxious.

As I mentioned in the first couple of cases after my move to Florida, sleep was impossible. Recurring nightmares, featuring Barrow hanging in all kinds of places, would keep me up at nights. Sometimes, there were dozens of him hanging. It was maddening, but in a weird way it felt like the price I had to pay for my failure to do the right thing.

Anyway, two weeks and a day after the suicide, Stone was out with an attack of the gout. We'd been working a cold case, but without him around, I was snooping around the Mercury case. Looking over the case file, I saw a friend of a friend of Mary's who we never spoke to.

It was a long shot, but I had to know if Barrow did it or not. I grabbed my parka, and on the way out, the phone rang.

"Detective Frank Luca, Homicide."

"This is Detective Ron Santo, Keansburg. You have a minute?"

"Sure, Ron. What's up."

"We arrested a male last night by the name of Peter Wilcox. New York has a warrant for him. They want him on a murder charge."

"Wow. How'd you'd grab him?"

"We caught him trying to drag a girl under the pier. We believe he's the predator we've been looking for."

"Good work. What can I do for you?"

"Before we hand him over to New York, I thought you should talk to him."

"Why's that?"

"He's claiming to know something about the Mercury case, the one where the kid hanged himself."

Like I needed the reminder. "What exactly?"

"He's hinting that he did it. Seems like he's looking to make some kind of a deal."

"I'll be right down."

Driving along Route 35, I didn't know what kind of result I desired. Deep down, I wanted the truth to come out. The problem was living with it if it turned out that Barrow hadn't killed Mary. Would I ever be able to sleep?

I pushed through the doors of the Keansburg police station, shoving aside the personal repercussions. I'd had a duty to see it through.

Chapter Twenty-Five

My stomach was doing flips as I walked into the office. I'd just returned from attending a lineup at the Keansburg Police Department. I had information to share.

Stone was on the phone, and the fax machine was whirring. I grabbed a sheet out of the tray as Stone finished his call. It was from the lab. When he hung up, I said, "O'Rourke identified Wilcox as the man she saw in Poricy Park. And the lab report just came in. The fiber under Mary's fingernail matches Wilcox's jacket. He's the killer."

To me it was a mere formality. Wilcox knew Mary didn't have her pocketbook and told us where he'd dumped it. But Stone took it hard. He was taking a lot of heat from the brass. To his credit, he told Gesso that I had my doubts about the case. The gesture almost made me feel bad for him.

Stone slumped in his chair. "They couldn't have caught this bastard after I was out of here?"

"Trust me, knowing all this doesn't make me feel any better. In fact, it's worse. But the bottom line is Barrow didn't kill Mary, it was Wilcox."

"Damn it."

"You want me to tell Gesso?"

"Nah, I gotta do it."

"I have say, he really stepped up by handling the parents. I hope knowing their son was innocent dulls their pain."

"They're also talking a settlement with them."

"Whatever they get, they deserve."

If they got twenty million, I'm sure some jerk would invoke the *good coming out of bad* phrase.

FOR MONTHS, I tried to figure out why Barrow had lied about being in the park. I knew I was looking for a reason to blame the kid for what happened to assuage the guilt that gnawed at me.

Try as hard as I did, I couldn't come up with anything more than there was someone who looked like Barrow. They say everybody has a double, and I'd been mistaken for George Clooney several times but it never felt right.

I finally realized that no other reason needed to exist. The power to prevent, or at least protest, the arrest that led to Barrow's suicide was in my hands and I flubbed it. I bore a lot of responsibility and swore that I'd never compromise my beliefs.

When something was wrong or didn't fit, I was going to say something, no matter the consequences. If we didn't have more than enough evidence on a suspect, there was no way I'd sign off on an arrest. I'd walk away from the job if it came to it.

From that case forward, I had to be a 1000 percent sure about who I arrested for murder. It went even deeper than arresting someone. We had a lot power, and casting the impression someone was involved in a crime had an impact beyond what I thought possible.

It might have been a rare reaction, but Barrow killed himself out of an anguish of suspicion. Something like the Barrow case was never going to happen again. Never.

You know, maybe there is a little bit of truth to that *good coming out of bad* saying after all.

The End

Thank you for reading, ***The Barrow Case: A Luca Mystery Prequel.*** We hope you enjoyed this book and will work your way into the full series. You can find a complete list of the authors work on the following pages, and on his website where you can subscribe for his newsletter of future books, story insights, and on very rare occasions special deals and recommendations.

www.danpetrosini.com

THE LUCA MYSTERY SERIES

THE BARROW CASE

AM I THE KILLER

VANISHED

THE SERENITY MURDER

THIRD CHANCES

A COLD, HARD CASE

COP OR KILLER?

SILENCING SALTER

A KILLER MISSTEPS

UNCERTAIN STAKES

THE GRANDPA KILLER

DANGEROUS REVENGE

WHERE ARE THEY

BURIED AT THE LAKE

THE PRESERVE KILLER

NO ONE IS SAFE

MURDER, MONEY AND MAYHEM

THE GOLDEN SELLOUT

THE WATERSIDE SECRET

SUSPENSEFUL SECRETS

CORY'S DILEMMA

CORY'S FLIGHT

CORY'S SHIFT

Dan is a USA Today and Amazon best-selling author who wrote his first story at the age of ten and enjoys telling a story or joke.

Dan gets his story ideas by exploring the question; What if?

In almost every situation he finds himself in, Dan explores what if this or that happened? What if this person died or did something unusual or illegal?

Dan's non-stop mind spin provides him with plenty of material to weave into interesting stories.

A fan of books and films that have twists and are difficult to predict, Dan crafts his stories to prevent readers from guessing correctly. He writes every day, forcing the words out when necessary and has written over twenty-five novels to date.

It's not a matter of wanting to write, Dan simply has to.

Dan passionately believes people can realize their dreams if they focus and act, and he encourages just that.

His favorite saying is – "The price of discipline is always less than the cost of regret"

Dan reminds people to get the negativity out of their lives. He believes it is contagious and advises people to steer clear of negative people. He knows having a true, positive mind set makes it feel like life is rigged in your favor. When he gets off base, he tells himself, 'You can't have a good day with a bad attitude.'

Married with two daughters and a needy Maltese, Dan lives in Southwest Florida. A New York native, Dan has taught at local colleges, writes novels, and plays tenor saxophone in several jazz bands. He also drinks way too much wine and never, ever takes himself too seriously.

He puts out a twice-a-month newsletter featuring articles, his writing and special deals and steals.

Sign up at www.danpetrosini.com